THE MATH KIDS:
THE PRIME-TIME BURGLARS

DAVID COLE

COMMON DEER PRESS

WWW.COMMONDEERPRESS.COM

Published by Common Deer Press Incorporated.

Published in 2018 by Common Deer Press
3203-1 Scott St.
Toronto, ON
M5V 1A1

This book is a work of fiction. Names, characters,
places, and incidents are either the product of the
author's imagination or are used fictitiously.

Library of Congress Cataloging-in-Publication Data
Cole, David.-First edition.
The Math Kids: The Prime-Time Burglars / David Cole
ISBN: 978-1-988761-22-0 (print)
ISBN: 978-1-988761-23-7 (e-book)

Cover Image: © Shannon O'Toole
Book Design: Ellie Sipila
Printed in Canada

WWW.COMMONDEERPRESS.COM

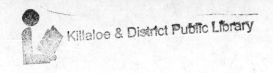

THE MATH KIDS: THE PRIMETIME BURGLARS

FOR ALL THOSE KIDS WHO LOOK
FORWARD TO MATH CLASS.
THE FUTURE BELONGS TO YOU

CHAPTER 1

E verything changed the afternoon she marched into our fourth-grade classroom, her black ponytail bouncing in rhythm with her footsteps.

"Hi everyone, I'm Stephanie," she announced from the front of the room.

I looked on in amazement. Here she was, a new kid in a new school where she didn't know anybody, and she walked in like she owned the place. *That is so cool*, I thought, wishing I had that kind of confidence.

For the first time that day, our teacher Mrs. Gouche smiled, and you could almost feel some of the tension from the morning easing.

"Class, this is Stephanie Lewis," she said. She looked down at the paperwork Stephanie had brought with her. "Her family just moved here from California. Stephanie's favorite subject is math and she loves to play soccer. I hope everyone will make her feel welcome. Stephanie, please take an empty desk. I'm sure you're going to love it here."

Stephanie smiled and made her way toward the empty desk right in front of mine. The first spitball hit her before she got halfway there. That's when Mrs. Grouch appeared.

When Mrs. Gouche was having a rough day, she sometimes snapped and her alter ego, who we called Mrs. Grouch, appeared. None of us were brave enough to call her that to her face, of course, except maybe Robbie Colson, who usually spent at least two days a week staying after school for detention.

"THAT'S IT!" she yelled, and the room became instantly silent.

To be fair, it wasn't really Mrs. Gouche's fault she was angry. It was after lunch by the time Stephanie arrived, and Mrs. Gouche had already been having a frustrating day. Robbie Colson and his band of bullies, which mostly consisted of Bill Cape and Bryce Bookerman, had been giving her a hard time all morning.

It had started just five minutes into the day when the dry erase markers went missing.

"Has anyone seen the markers?" she had asked. When no one answered, her eyes moved to Robbie. Even with no evidence, Robbie was a pretty good bet if you had to pick someone who had done something wrong.

"Don't look at me," he protested. "Why do you always think it's me?"

"Perhaps because it usually is, Robbie," she replied. "Are you sure you don't know anything about the markers?"

"How do you know someone didn't hide them in their desk?" Bryce asked.

"Yeah, I think I saw Susie playing with them a few minutes ago," Bill chimed in.

Susie McDonald had a look of shock on her face.

"Can you check your desk, please, Susie?" the teacher asked.

"But I didn't—" Susie started.

"I understand you didn't put them there, but can you please check?"

Susie opened the lid to her desk.

"It doesn't look like they're here, Mrs. Gouche," she said with a sigh of relief.

"Try looking under her social studies book," Robbie said to the teacher with an attempt at an innocent look.

Susie lifted the book and there they were. All the color drained from her face, and her shoulders shook as she started to sob. She looked like she might be ill at any moment.

"You three seem to know quite a bit about the inside of Susie's desk," Mrs. Gouche said, looking pointedly at the bullies as she put an arm around Susie's shoulders to console her.

The bullies protested, but I could see that our teacher wasn't buying any of it. It looked like another detention was in store for them.

"Jordan, can you walk Susie down to the nurse?" Mrs. Gouche asked.

"Me?"

"Yes, you, Jordan Waters. Or is there another Jordan in the room I don't know about?" she asked.

"No, ma'am," I answered lamely.

I walked Susie down the hall. I wasn't sure if I was supposed to go back, so I stood outside the nurse's office reading the health bulletin board until I heard my name being called. I looked down the hall and saw my best friend, Justin Grant, coming my way.

"You get lost coming back to class?" he asked.

"I was hoping to stay out here until English is over," I answered with a smile. "If I can stall until lunch then it's math class this afternoon."

I was a whiz in math and I loved to read, but I wasn't so good when it came to writing and spelling. Justin gave me trouble about this sometimes, but I didn't let it bother me since he's been my best friend since kindergarten.

"We'd better get back before Mrs. Gouche sends out a search party," Justin said. "If Robbie and his friends keep it up, there's no telling when Mrs. Grouch is going to show up."

I nodded glumly and slouched back to the classroom.

The rest of the morning had gone just as badly for Mrs. Gouche. It wasn't just the bullies either. Everyone seemed to be on edge and snapping at each other. But it was that spitball hitting Stephanie that finally put her over the edge.

Stephanie was still standing next to my desk. She had frozen in place when Mrs. Gouche yelled. I wondered what she had to be thinking—*two minutes into my new classroom, and the teacher has already lost it.*

Mrs. Gouche stared at everyone in the class, but saved her sternest looks for Robbie, Bill, and Bryce. Even Robbie wasn't brave enough to return that look. Instead, he pretended to be searching for something in his desk. Mrs. Gouche didn't say anything for a moment but you could tell she was thinking about her next step. What price would be paid for the day she had been through?

She decided to take her frustration out on the whole class. Why do teachers do that? I didn't hide the markers or shoot the spitball, so why should I be punished? If you want to know the truth, I think Mrs. Gouche was just looking for an hour of silence when she hatched her evil plan.

"Everyone get out a pencil and a sheet of paper. I'm giving you an assignment," she said, her eyebrows dropping into a sharp *v*.

The class responded with groans and frowns. Before Robbie could even open his mouth, Mrs. Gouche turned to him and said, "And if you say one word, Robbie Colson, one single word, I'll be on the phone with your parents before that word even reaches my ear. Is that understood?"

I hoped that he would say *yes*. I wanted to see if that counted as saying one word. But Robbie just nodded his head in silence. No kid, not even a member of Robbie's band of thugs, wanted a call made to their parents. Detention was nothing compared to what your parents could do to you.

"Here is your assignment. I want you to add up all the numbers from 1 to 100," she said with something like an evil grin. "No calculators and *no talking* while you are working," she added. "And be sure to check your answer before you bring it to me."

In stunned silence, I took out a sheet of paper and started to work.

$$1 + 2 = 3$$
$$3 + 3 = 6$$
$$6 + 4 = 10$$
$$10 + 5 = 15$$

This is terrible. It's going to take forever, I thought. *What a lousy way to spend an afternoon—and I like math!* I wondered what the kids who didn't were thinking.

I'd only added the first five numbers when Stephanie rose from her chair and approached Mrs. Gouche, who was leaning back contentedly in her chair.

Mrs. Gouche was startled to see Stephanie standing in front of her with a piece of paper in her hand.

"What is it, Stephanie?" she asked.

"I'm finished, ma'am," Stephanie said with a smile.

Everyone in the classroom put their pencils down and watched the interaction.

"You added all of the numbers from 1 to 100?" Mrs. Gouche asked.

"Yes, ma'am," Stephanie responded.

"All one hundred numbers?"

"Yes, ma'am."

"And you're certain your answer is correct?"

"Yes, ma'am," Stephanie replied politely.

"And what's the answer?"

"5,050."

"That's impossible!"

"Impossible?"

"There's no way you could have added all of those numbers in less than a minute!" Mrs. Gouche said angrily. "You just made up a number."

"Want to bet a class pizza party on it?" Stephanie asked as her lips curved into a sly smile.

"You're on!" Mrs. Gouche growled.

The class watched as the teacher began to punch numbers into her calculator. "Staring at me isn't going to get you the right answer," she said to the class. "Get back to work!"

Forty minutes later, Mrs. Gouche stared at her calculator in disbelief. The number 5,050 stared back at her in glowing green digits.

Man, that pizza is going to taste great. I gave Stephanie a big grin as she returned to her seat.

"How did you do that?" I whispered.

"I'll show you after school," she replied.

And that's when the idea for the math club popped into my head. At the time, I had no idea where that idea would take us.

CHAPTER 2

Robbie, Bill, and Bryce were in detention for hiding the dry erase markers in Susie's desk. The rest of the class had gone home except for Justin, Stephanie, and me. Justin and I listened in wonder as Stephanie explained how she had added the numbers from 1 to 100 so quickly.

"It was really pretty easy," she said. "Let me show you."

She went to the board and began to write as she explained.

"You see, I just put all of the numbers into pairs that would add up to 100. I put 1 with 99, 2 with 98, 3 with 97, and so on, all the way up to 49 and 51. That gave me 49 pairs that each added up to 100, so that was 4,900. The only numbers that didn't have a pair were 100 and 50, so I just added those at the end. 4,900 plus 100 plus 50 equals 5,050."

"That's amazing," Justin said in awe.

I should tell you that that's high praise coming from Justin, who isn't amazed by too many things. He's one of the smartest kids I've ever met, so when he says something is amazing, it probably is.

"I'm just glad that she didn't ask us to add up the numbers from 1 to 1,000," Stephanie remarked.

"That's for sure," I said. "But…"

"But what?" Justin asked.

"Well, if your trick worked for the numbers from 1 to 100, why not for 1 to 1,000?" I asked.

"I guess it should," Stephanie said thoughtfully.

Justin didn't respond, but he was already writing on the board.

$$1 + 999 = 1,000$$
$$2 + 998 = 1,000$$
$$3 + 997 = 1,000$$
$$...$$
$$499 + 501 = 1,000$$

"We'll have 499 groups of 1,000, so that would be 499,000," Justin said.

"And don't forget to add the 500 and 1,000 'cause they don't have a pair." I added.

"So the answer will be 500,500," Stephanie said.

The three of us stared at the board. Someone with really good hearing might have actually heard the wheels turning in our heads.

"That's amazing," Justin said for the second time. "That means we could do the same thing for any group of numbers, couldn't we?"

It wasn't really a question. You see, Justin is always thinking ahead. He doesn't want to just learn something.

He wants to really learn it and then figure out other ways to use it. My dad would call him someone who thinks outside the box, but I'd go a little further than that. I'd call Justin a guy who thinks outside the entire room.

Fifteen minutes later, the board was filled with calculations. We had added the numbers from 1 to 10,000, from 1 to 100,000, and even from 1 to 1,000,000.

It wasn't until we were done and had written all the answers on the board that we saw something even more unbelievable. As usual, Justin saw it first.

1 to 100	5,050
1 to 1,000	500,500
1 to 10,000	50,005,000
1 to 100,000	5,000,050,000
1 to 1,000,000	500,000,500,000

"That's amazing," Justin said for the third time in an hour, which had to be a new world record for him. "Do you see the pattern?" he asked.

Stephanie and I looked for a moment, and then there it was. When we added the numbers from 1 to 1,000, the answer was 500 followed by another 500. For 1 to 10,000, the answer was 5,000 followed by another 5,000.

"So, we could do this for any group of numbers without even having to add up all of the pairs," Stephanie said. "The answer is just half the number written twice."

She started to go on but was interrupted by a voice in the doorway.

"Well, isn't this cute. Nerds doing math." Robbie leaned against the doorframe, his arms crossed. His large body was blocking the way to the hall, and Bill and Bryce peered over his shoulders.

"Here's some math for you— teacher's pet times three equals nerds," Bill chimed in.

Robbie and Bryce laughed as if it was the funniest joke they'd ever heard.

"And you, new girl, it's your fault we got detention," Robbie snarled.

"My name is Stephanie. And let me see if I've got this straight." She raised a forefinger. "Somehow it's my fault that your spitball managed to hit me, even with your pitiful aim?"

Robbie stared at Stephanie without saying a word. His fists balled up at his sides as his face began to turn a purplish red color. He took two steps toward us, followed closely by Bryce and Bill. This wasn't good. Not good at all.

"Hey, what are you kids still doing here? Didn't get enough learning for one day?" It was the loud, happy voice of the school janitor, Old Mike. He wasn't really that old, but that was what everyone called him. *Old Mike will take care of that spill. Ask Old Mike where you can get a new pencil sharpener. Make sure Old Mike locks up the back door when he's done cleaning for the night.*

I didn't care what they called him. I just knew I was never so happy to see him.

"We were just leaving," I said quickly.

Before I lost the chance, I walked past Robbie, hopping to avoid the foot I knew he would stick out to try to trip me. And then we were past the three bullies and into the hallway.

"Have a great day, Old Mike," I called back as we hustled down the hall, leaving a trio of scowling faces behind us.

We were safe for now, but I had a bad feeling that we weren't going to get off that easy. I clenched my teeth. Fourth grade is hard enough without bullies drawing a target on your back.

We walked home together. We figured there was safety in numbers, although I didn't know how many people I would need to feel safe around Robbie and his buddies. It turned out that Stephanie's family had moved to the street right behind ours, so she was only about four houses away if you cut through back yards. Justin was across the street from me and five houses down, so I was almost exactly in the middle of the three of us.

"That was really cool what you did with that addition trick," I said as we stopped in front of Stephanie's house. "I bet you'll be in the yellow math group with us starting tomorrow."

"Good. My last school was pretty boring most of the time. We didn't have different math groups, so there wasn't the chance to work at our own speed," Stephanie replied.

"And it wasn't really a trick, you know," she added. "It was just looking at the numbers a little differently."

Justin nodded his head and said, "Mm-hmm," but you could tell he was thinking. That isn't unusual for Justin. He is always thinking about something. And when he's deep in thought, he always replies *mm-hmm* to anything you say. I sometimes make it into a game and try to guess what he's thinking about, but I'm hardly ever right. Once, on the way to school, we were talking about baseball when he went suddenly silent. In my head, I tried to figure out what problem he was trying to solve. Was he calculating the batting average of the Washington National's best hitter? Was he trying to figure out the odds of a team making the playoffs when they were five games out of first with only eight games to play? It turns out I wasn't even close. He was trying to figure out how he could defeat the troll on level three of the latest video game he was playing.

"Justin, do you want to eat at my house tonight?" I asked. "We're having fried worms."

Stephanie gave me a questioning look, but Justin merely replied, "Mm-hmm."

Yes, he was definitely deep in thought. I gave him a few seconds to finish thinking, and when he looked around like he wasn't sure how he had gotten here, I knew he was back. I never did find out what he was thinking about because I chose that time to make my suggestion.

"We should start a math club," I said.

"A math club?" Justin asked.

"Yeah. We could work on tricky math problems. My dad has a lot of cool math books and puzzles. Maybe we could even enter some math competitions as a team," I said.

"Count me in!" Stephanie said, nodding her head. Her ponytail bobbed up and down with each nod.

"I'm in too," Justin added.

"We could meet on Saturday mornings, and we—" I began.

"Um, Saturday mornings aren't good for me," Stephanie said. "I have soccer practice."

"Well, when is soccer season over?" Justin asked.

"It's never really over," she replied. "There's a fall season, then the winter indoor soccer league, then spring season. And then there are camps during the summer, which are usually mostly drills but still fun and a good way..."

"We get it. What you're saying is that you're stuck playing soccer every Saturday." Justin interrupted.

"Pretty much," she said, twisting her ponytail tightly around her finger. "But I don't think of it as being stuck. I really love playing soccer."

"Sounds like being stuck to me," Justin said.

I stepped in to try to salvage the situation. I didn't want to see the math club dissolve before it even got started.

"How about Saturday afternoons? Would that work for everyone?"

Stephanie and her ponytail nodded vigorously. We both looked at Justin. He took a long pause and then nodded. The club was on!

CHAPTER 3

O kay, what should we call ourselves?" Stephanie
asked.

"How about, the Math Kids?" Justin said.

"That's perfect!" said Stephanie. "It says just what
we are and isn't cutesy. I hate cutesy."

I had been about to suggest the Three Mathketeers,
as another option, which is about as cutesy as it gets,
but instead I bit my lip and said "Yeah, that would
work."

"And Jordan should be president, since it was his
idea!" Stephanie said.

Justin seconded that opinion, and just like that we
had a club, a name, and a president.

We decided to have our first official meeting at my
house on Saturday afternoon. We all decided to bring
some of our favorite math puzzles. Stephanie said she
would bring double-stuffed Oreos. I agreed to supply
the milk. With all the club necessities figured out, we
dropped Stephanie off at her house and I walked the

rest of the way home with Justin, cutting through the Greenfeld's back yard on the way.

"You know, Stephanie's not bad. For a girl, I mean," I said as Justin left me at my door.

"Yeah, I guess," he said without much commitment. I watched him walk away. *He'll come around*, I thought. *Just wait until the first meeting*. The combination of Stephanie's math skills and her double-stuffed Oreos would be the winning ticket.

The timing for our first meeting turned out to be perfect because we were about to get the first real challenge as the Math Kids.

"I'm home," I yelled as I walked through the mudroom, as if the sound of the slamming door and my backpack getting thrown into my cubby weren't loud enough to announce my presence.

"I'll alert the media," my sister, Linda, said sarcastically from the family room. I could hear one of her stupid shows on the TV.

"That's about as funny as a screen door in a submarine," I shot back.

"That joke is as old as grandma's bathrobe," she replied.

"You should know since you smell like her bathrobe." My comeback didn't make much sense, but it was always important to get the last insult in.

That was a typical conversation for my older sister and me. Linda was in middle school now and thought she was too cool to be seen with me in public, but at home with no one around she wasn't so bad. We teased each other incessantly, but I knew she'd always be there for me if I needed her. She had gotten me out of trouble more than once with my parents, so I guess I owed her.

"Where's Mom?" I asked.

"Upstairs, I think."

"More importantly—"

"—when's dinner?" Linda interrupted, finishing my sentence for me.

"You know me too good." I laughed.

"*Well*," my mother said as she entered the room.

"Well what?" I said in confusion.

"You know me too *well*," she said.

Now I was really confused. "Of course I know you."

"You are such a doofus," my sister said. "She means that it should be *you know me too well* instead of *you know me too good*."

As I've said before, I am really good at math, but I'm a complete flop when it comes to English. I'm clueless about when to when to use *good* or *well*, or whether it's *their*, *they're*, or there. My sister and my mom are always correcting me, but my dad cuts me some slack. He shares my love of all things math. He is a mechanical engineer and always says that you can't be good at everything, so you might as well be good at something important—like math!

"Okay, you know me too well," I said. "But seriously—"

"—when's dinner?" my sister finished my sentence with a grin.

"How did you know that's what he was going to say?" My mother laughed.

"It's not too tough to figure it out when that's the first thing out of his mouth every day when he walks in the door," Linda explained.

"That's not true," I argued as I headed for the pantry to see if I could find something to eat. "Sometimes I ask what's for dinner instead of when's dinner."

"Jordan, don't go filling up on junk food right before we eat," my mom said.

"But I'm starving," I responded.

"I think you can hold out for another thirty minutes."

"How about if I just have a couple of graham crackers?"

"Two."

"How about four?" I asked.

"Three, and that's it."

My mom and I had that same conversation almost every day when I came home from school. I said I was hungry. She said to wait for dinner. I asked for graham crackers or some other snack. We bargained on the number. That was alright though. She almost never bargained me down lower than I wanted to go, and I suppose I never got more than she wanted me to have, so in the end it worked out okay for everybody.

I munched on my graham crackers and had a glass of milk while my mom bustled around the kitchen preparing dinner. She was reading a recipe off of her iPad while she worked. She was making some kind of casserole thing that was full of spinach and vegetables. It even smelled green. It made me wish I'd tried to bargain for a few more graham crackers.

I had finished my snack and managed to get my glass into the sink with only one reminder from my mom when I heard the garage door go up and I knew my dad was home. Sometimes he'd play catch with me before dinner, but he seemed engrossed in the evening newspaper, so I didn't ask him this time.

"Another burglary," he said as he turned the page in the paper. "That's the third one this week. They seem to be getting bolder too. The woman was at home and they stole a purse right off of the kitchen table."

"She's lucky she wasn't hurt," my mom said without lifting her eyes from her iPad.

Twenty minutes later, I was poking at my dinner, trying to avoid some of the grosser veggies, when Linda came up with the first challenge for the Math Kids.

It didn't start as a math problem, but that's where it ended up.

"Daddy," Linda said—

I knew right away that she wanted something. When a sentence started with *Daddy*, it was usually followed by *I want* or *can I*. And that was true in this case.

—"can I have some friends over to celebrate my birthday next week?" she asked.

"Like a party?" my dad asked.

"No, more like a little dinner. I was thinking Mom could help me make lasagna and cheesy garlic bread, and maybe some cheesecake for dessert!" Linda said excitedly.

"That's a pretty cheesy meal isn't it?" My dad smiled.

"Everything she does is cheesy," I added, drawing a frown of disapproval from my mother and a stuck-out tongue from my sister.

"I think we could make that happen," said my mom. "How many are you inviting?"

"I was thinking of inviting seven, so there would be eight people altogether," Linda responded. She ticked names off on her fingers while she listed potential attendants. "Me, Amy, Brad, Beth, Charles, Debbie, Emily, and Frances."

"A boy girl party, huh? I thought we had decided no boy girl parties until eighth grade," my dad said with raised eyebrows.

"But it's not a party. It's a dinner. That's different," Linda argued.

"Sounds like a party to me," I argued back, drawing a second stuck-out tongue from my sister.

"Well, I suppose we could give it a try," Mom said. "But everybody stays in the kitchen the whole time."

"I was hoping we could use the dining room," Linda said, giving Dad her best pleading look.

"Okay, then everybody stays in the dining room the whole time," he said.

"Hope nobody has to go to the bathroom." I snorted. "That would make a real mess in the dining room." That comment cost me doing the dishes that night, but it was worth it.

The discussion continued for a couple of minutes, but I had lost interest in the dinner, or party, or whatever it was, by then. Instead, I was thinking about the first math club meeting the next day. What were we going to take on as our first math challenge? It was then that my sister unknowingly answered the question.

"Now, all I need to do is figure out where everyone is going to sit," she said.

"It's a round table, so why does it matter where you sit?" my dad asked.

"It's not as easy as you think, Dad," Linda said. "I want to make sure I'm sitting by Amy since she's my best friend. Brad and Beth are kind of going out, so I know they'll want to sit next to each other, but Amy and I don't want to sit next to them while they're making goo-goo eyes at each other. Frances will want to sit next to Debbie. Amy doesn't want to sit next to Charles since he wouldn't dance with her at the summer dance, so I want to sit Charles next to either Debbie or Emily, but that's going to make one of them mad, so Debbie and Emily can't sit next to each other. Charles and Frances don't like Brad, so I can't put either of them next to him."

My mom and dad stared in amazement either at how complicated a simple birthday dinner could be or the fact that my sister could keep all of that information in her head.

I looked at Linda and made a bold announcement. "I can solve that problem for you, Linda."

Linda looked a little unsure.

"Trust me, I can do it," I said. "If you can write down all the rules for who has to sit with who and who can't sit with who, I'll help you to arrange your table."

And with that, the Math Kids had their first problem to solve.

WAIT! DO YOU WANT TO TRY TO SOLVE THIS PUZZLE BEFORE SEEING IF THE MATH KIDS CAN DO IT? TRY TO FIND A WAY TO SEAT EIGHT PEOPLE AROUND THE TABLE FOLLOWING THESE RULES:

AMY AND LINDA HAVE TO SIT TOGETHER

BRAD AND BETH HAVE TO SIT TOGETHER

CHARLES HAS TO SIT BY EITHER DEBBIE OR EMILY

FRANCES HAS TO SIT BY DEBBIE

AMY AND LINDA CAN'T SIT BY BRAD OR BETH

CHARLES CAN'T SIT BY BRAD

FRANCES CAN'T SIT BY BRAD

DEBBIE AND EMILY CAN'T SIT TOGETHER

AMY CAN'T SIT BY CHARLES

THERE MAY BE MORE THAN ONE RIGHT ANSWER. GOOD LUCK!

CHAPTER 4

T hat's not really a math problem, is it?" Stephanie asked as we settled into chairs in my dad's home office. It was a great place for us to work since it had a large rolling white board.

Stephanie was right. My sister's dinner party was more of a logic problem than a math problem, but I still wanted it to be the Math Kids first challenge. I guess I wanted it because it was a real life problem, not just something out of a book. Luckily, Justin came to my rescue.

"I think it is," he said. "Logic is about using reasoning."

"And math is about operations using numbers," Stephanie countered.

"True," Justin argued, "but when early mathematicians found math things they couldn't understand they used logic to figure it out. So, without logic we wouldn't have a lot of the math we have today."

Stephanie thought about this for a moment and nodded. "Okay, let's do it," she said.

Yes! Our first challenge as a team!

"What are the rules?" Justin asked.

I wrote them out on my dad's white board in my sloppy but readable handwriting:

Amy and Linda have to sit together
Brad and Beth have to sit together
Charles has to sit by either Debbie or Emily
Frances has to sit by Debbie
Amy and Linda can't sit by Brad or Beth
Charles can't sit by Brad
Frances can't sit by Brad
Debbie and Emily can't sit together
Amy can't sit by Charles

"What is wrong with these people?" Stephanie asked.

Justin and I broke into laughter. These rules were a little silly, but I still didn't care because this was our first test.

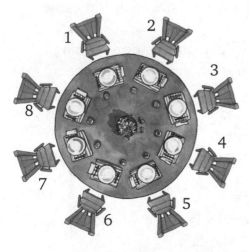

"Okay, what's our first step?" I asked. I had a few ideas of my own, but I wanted to make sure we worked together on solving this.

"We should—" Stephanie began.

"We need to be able to see the problem better," Justin interrupted.

Stephanie was already on her feet in front of the white board. She drew a circle to show the table, with eight boxes around the circle to represent the chairs.

"What are the numbers for?" Justin asked. "It's a circle, so it doesn't really matter where they sit."

"I thought if we give each chair a number, it would be easier to keep track," she said.

"Yeah, I guess that makes sense," Justin said a little reluctantly. Still, I could tell that he was really getting into it. Our first challenge looked like it was going to be a hit.

"Okay, we're off to a great start!" I said.

And then there was silence. Stephanie, Justin, and I stared at the board, our eyes moving back and forth between the rules and the picture of the table.

"What do you think, Justin?" I asked.

Justin responded with his usual "Mm-hmm," and I knew his mind was hard at work.

"What if we started with putting Linda and Amy at chairs 1 and 2?" I suggested.

"That makes sense," Stephanie agreed. "Like Justin said, since it's a round table, it doesn't really matter what position we put them at, so 1 and 2 are just as good as any other spots."

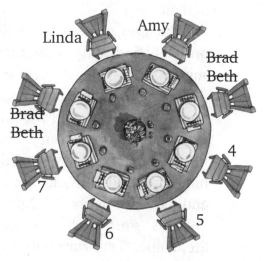

"And since they don't want to sit by Beth and Brad, we know Brad and Beth aren't at spots 3 or 8," Justin added.

Stephanie put Linda and Amy in their assigned spots and noted where Brad and Beth couldn't be seated.

"Okay, now we're getting somewhere," I said.

At least I thought we were getting somewhere. After that first burst of inspiration, we hit a roadblock. We looked at the rules and the picture of the table, but no one could figure out where to go from there.

"I've got an idea," Stephanie said.

Justin and I looked up hopefully.

"What is it?" I asked.

"Cookies!" she shouted.

I had to laugh. Her excitement was contagious. And, after all, who could argue with cookies?

We munched on Oreo cookies and drank large glasses of ice-cold milk while we stared at the white board. Somewhere in the middle of a large bite, Justin had an idea.

"Since no one seems to like Brad, I think we can probably find some other spots where he can't sit," he suggested.

That makes sense, I thought. I also wondered why no one wanted to sit by Brad. I didn't even know the guy, but I felt a little sorry for him. I remembered a kid in first grade, Tommy something, who always sat by himself. I used to think about asking him to join Justin and me, but I never did. Now I kind of wish I had.

"Let's start finding places Brad can't sit," said Stephanie. "Let's start with spot 4."

"Okay, if Brad was at spot 4, who can sit in spot 3?" Justin asked.

It turned out to be a great question.

"If Brad sat in spot 4, then we can eliminate Charles and Frances from spot 3, since they didn't want to sit by Brad," I said. "That only leaves Debbie or Emily."

"And it can't be Debbie, because she has to sit by Frances, so that only leaves Emily," Stephanie said excitedly.

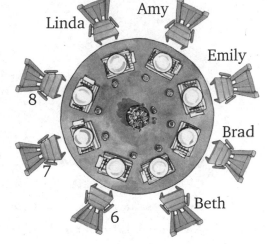

"Where does that leave us?" Justin asked.

Stephanie updated the picture with Brad in spot 4, Beth in spot 5, and Emily in spot 3.

We were getting close, unless of course we were wrong about Brad being in spot 4.

"If we're right, that only leaves Charles, Frances, and Debbie," I said.

"Debbie has to be in spot 7!" Stephanie said excitedly.

"How do you know?" I asked.

"Easy," said Justin. "Debbie needs to sit by both Frances and Charles, so she has to be in the middle of them."

"And I think we can put Frances and Charles in either of spots 6 or 8," I said.

Stephanie completed the picture and we all stared

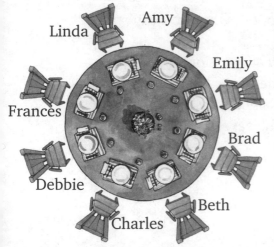

at it, then back at the rules, then back at the picture of the table.

I could tell that everyone was running through each of the rules to make sure our answer was right. Stephanie made it official by putting a check mark by each rule as she made sure our answer worked.

Amy and Linda have to sit together ✓
Brad and Beth have to sit together ✓
Charles has to sit by either Debbie or Emily ✓
Frances has to sit by Debbie ✓
Amy and Linda can't sit by Brad or Beth ✓
Charles can't sit by Brad ✓
Frances can't sit by Brad ✓
Debbie and Emily can't sit together ✓
Amy can't sit by Charles ✓

We had done it. We had solved the problem. Linda's dinner party was saved. Stephanie was happily eating a cookie to celebrate our victory. Only Justin was silent, a slight frown on his face.

"What's wrong, Justin?" I asked.

"Mm-hmm," he responded.

I ate my own cookie and gave him a minute to finish

processing his thoughts. I didn't even try to guess what he was thinking this time.

"It's not right," he said.

"It is right," Stephanie insisted. "We checked every rule."

"I know, but it's not right," Justin said.

"What's wrong?" I asked.

"There's more than one answer to the problem."

"So?" I asked.

"That's very un-mathy," he said.

"Un-mathy?" Stephanie asked. "Is that even a word?"

It probably wasn't a word. But I understood what Justin was saying. We were used to math having a single answer. 4 plus 4 always equals 8. You would never hear someone saying that 4 plus 4 could also equal 7 or a 143. In fact, that was one of the things I really liked about math. It wasn't like English where there were lots of words that sounded alike but meant something totally different. That seemed like a real waste (or was that "waist"?) and it just made it harder for me to pass our weekly spelling test.

"I don't care if it's a word or not," Justin snapped. "Math doesn't work that way."

That's when Stephanie stepped in to save the day.

"Actually, it does," she said.

"What do you mean?" Justin asked.

"What number can you multiply by itself to get 4?"

"That's easy," Justin said. "2."

"Is that it?" Stephanie asked.

Justin thought for a second. "-2 also works," he said. Stephanie was right! There were math problems that had more than one answer. I quickly thought of another.

"Yeah, and what about zero times x equals zero?" I asked. "You can put any number in for x and the equation will be true."

And that's when he got it. Sometimes there *were* math problems that had more than one answer.

Justin looked thoughtful for a moment, and then nodded and reached for his glass of milk. He raised it in a toast.

"We did it! To the Math Kids!" he said with a grin.

We clinked our glasses together. We had succeeded in the first challenge of the Math Kids!

Unfortunately, our next challenge didn't go nearly as well.

CHAPTER 5

Monday started off on a good note. Over breakfast, my sister told me she owed me one for saving her party. On the way to school I was thinking about all the ways I could cash in on my sister's debt when I found some real cash, a five-dollar bill blown up against a fence. It looked like it was going to be a lucky day, but I was still shocked to see the *85%* written across the top of my spelling test. I was usually happy to get a 65, so an 85 was unheard of for me. I even checked Mrs. Gouche's math to make sure she had gotten it right. 17 out of 20—yeah, that was 85% alright. I couldn't wait to show my mom.

To make things even better, Robbie was absent from school. Without him, the class was spared any bullying for the day, since Bill and Bryce usually didn't start anything without their leader. Apparently Robbie was sick, but I suspected he was faking it. For being the biggest and strongest kid in the class, he sure missed a lot of school due to illness. I'd also decided he was one of the clumsiest kids I'd ever met. Once, he was out for almost a week when he ran his bike off the road and into a gully. He came back to class with his wrist in a sling, but that didn't stop him from using his one good arm to push the little kids around.

Overall, it was looking like a great Monday.

And that's when things started to fall apart.

As expected, Stephanie had been put into the yellow math group. That meant the Math Kids had a group to ourselves. Mrs. Gouche was going through some beginning algebra concepts. It was stuff Justin and I already knew, but I think Mrs. Gouche was trying to make sure Stephanie knew it too. Stephanie was getting bored with the lesson and wasn't making any secret of it. Finally, she came right out and said it.

"Mrs. Gouche, we already know this stuff," Stephanie began. "Can't we move on to something else?"

Mrs. Gouche gave Stephanie a look that Justin and I had come to know meant *you don't want to go there*, but Stephanie didn't catch on.

As Mrs. Gouche continued with the lesson, Stephanie interrupted.

"This is baby algebra," she said. "We were doing this at my school in California last year."

Mrs. Gouche looked at Stephanie. Justin and I looked at each other. We tried to signal to Stephanie that she should be quiet, but Stephanie had already shown us that she didn't back down from anything.

I tried to step in to help.

"Actually, this is a good review for me," I said, hoping to ease the tension.

"See, they already know it too," Stephanie said. "Can't you give us something more at our level?"

Justin looked down and shook his head. He knew Stephanie had gone too far, and now we would all pay the price. If there's one thing we'd learned, it's that teachers don't like to be questioned on their teaching methods.

"So, you're ready for something more difficult?" Mrs. Gouche asked. She asked the question nicely enough, but I could feel something else going on under the surface.

"Yes, ma'am," Stephanie responded. I could tell she felt pretty proud of herself.

"And you're sure you can solve more difficult problems?" Mrs. Gouche asked.

Stephanie nodded, but she seemed a little less sure of herself than she had been just a moment before. I think she was a little worried about the determined look on Mrs. Gouche's face. I know I was.

"Well, let's see if I can find something at your level," Mrs. Gouche said.

She walked to the board and drew a picture.

"This is the town of Königsberg," she explained. "There are four parts of the town, which I labeled A, B, C, and D. There are seven bridges in the town, which I numbered from 1 to 7. Your job is to visit each part of the town, going across every bridge exactly one time."

"Can we start wherever we want?" Justin asked.

Great question, I thought. Justin always seems to know just the right questions to ask. I usually just jump in and try to solve a puzzle, but Justin likes to do his thinking up front.

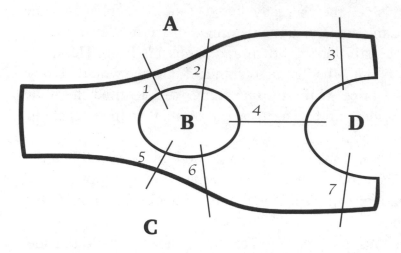

"Yes," Mrs. Gouche answered. "You can start wherever you want and you can go across the bridge from either side. You have to visit all parts of the town and you have to cross every bridge, but once you have crossed a bridge, you can't go across that same bridge again."

"Sounds pretty easy," Stephanie said.

"Think you could have it done by the end of class?" asked Mrs. Gouche.

"Absolutely!" Stephanie said.

"Care to bet a class pizza party on it?" Mrs. Gouche asked with a sly smile.

Before Justin and I could say anything, Stephanie had accepted the challenge. She smiled confidently, but I had a bad feeling about this.

WAIT! DO YOU WANT TO TRY TO SOLVE THIS PUZZLE BEFORE SEEING IF THE MATH KIDS CAN DO IT?

THE OLD TOWN OF KONIGSBERG HAS SEVEN BRIDGES. CAN YOU WALK THROUGH THE TOWN, VISITING EACH PART OF TOWN WHILE CROSSING EACH BRIDGE ONLY ONCE?

GOOD LUCK

An hour later, we hadn't made any progress. We came close a couple of times, but the answer remained just out of reach. We tried starting in each section of town, but the result was always the same. Every time, we either missed going over one of the bridges or were forced to recross one.

Mrs. Gouche watched our progress, that sly smile never leaving her face. I was right about that bad feeling.

There was a lot on the line, after all. By now the class had heard that we had bet the class pizza party. If we solved the problem, we would be heroes, with not one, but two pizza parties coming our way. If we failed, though… Well, I didn't want to think about what would happen if we couldn't solve it. Even though Robbie wasn't here, I still didn't want to see Bill and Bryce waiting for us outside the safety of the school building.

The clock ticked steadily toward three o'clock. As the minute hand approached the top of the hour, we worked faster and faster. We tried each starting point again, going across a different bridge to start. Still nothing. Justin made a chart on the board to make sure we weren't missing any combinations of starting points and bridges. Still nothing.

Eventually, our time ran out. The bell rang and class was over. The problem lay unsolved on the white board in front of us. We continued to stare at the board as our classmates filed out, many of them throwing wisecracks in our direction as they left.

"Nice job, nerds," Bill sneered.

"Just wait until Robbie hears about this," Bryce added, knocking a stack of papers off my desk as he passed.

Finally, it was just the four of us: Stephanie, Justin, Mrs. Gouche, and me.

"Was that problem a little above your level?" Mrs. Gouche asked Stephanie.

"I guess so," she responded quietly.

"I just can't believe we couldn't solve it," said Justin. "We tried every possible direction from every possible starting point."

"Are you sure?" Mrs. Gouche asked.

Justin looked carefully at his chart on the board and then nodded. "Yes, I'm sure we tried everything," he said.

"I meant, are you sure the problem can be solved?" she asked.

The thought had never crossed my mind. A problem with no answer? Had Mrs. Gouche tricked us?

While we thought about her question, Mrs. Gouche packed up her things and got ready to leave.

"Think about this. How many bridges go to area A?" she asked.

We looked. There were three bridges between area A and the other areas.

"What does that mean?" Mrs. Gouche asked.

We looked at her with puzzled looks on our faces.

"Let me ask that in a different way," she explained. "If you start in area A, where will you end up?"

We looked at the picture carefully. Stephanie was the one who came up with the answer.

"If you start at A, you would have to end up in some other area," she said. "Cross one bridge to leave, another to come back, and then the third to leave again."

"Right," said Mrs. Gauche. "And what happens if you start somewhere else and want to cross every bridge going to area A?"

We looked at the picture again and thought for a moment.

"You would have to end up in area A," I replied. "One bridge to get there, another to leave, and then the third to get to area A again."

"And what does that tell you?" Mrs. Gouche asked.

"It means we either need to start or end in area A," Justin answered.

"Correct," she nodded. "Now, there are also three bridges going to area C."

"That means we would either need to start or end in area C," Justin said, starting to see where Mrs. Gouche was going.

"And what about area D?"

And there it was. Area D also had three bridges, meaning we would have to start or end there too. It was impossible to start and end in three different places. Mrs. Gouche was right, the problem was impossible to solve!

"Please erase the white board when you're done," she called back to us as she left the room.

"She knew all along, didn't she?" Stephanie asked as the sound of Mrs. Gouche's footsteps faded down the hall.

"Mm-hmm," Justin said. It was the right answer to Stephanie's question, but he wasn't really answering. He was deep in thought once again. I couldn't even guess what he was thinking about. Over the weekend, we had solved a challenge with more than one answer. Now Mrs. Gouche had given us a problem that didn't even have an answer.

"We should have thought about it before betting the pizza party on it," Justin said, not even trying to disguise the irritation in his voice.

"I wouldn't have accepted the challenge if I didn't think I could do it," Stephanie snapped back.

"That's your problem, isn't it?"

"What's my problem?"

"You didn't think about the team, only about yourself."

I knew I needed to jump in before the argument got out of control.

"Hey guys, let's not be too hard on ourselves. That was a tough problem," I said.

"Not nearly as tough as the one we'll face tomorrow when Robbie gets back," Justin said.

Stephanie was deep in thought, nervously playing with the end of her ponytail.

CHAPTER 6

Justin was right. It did get worse when Robbie came back on Tuesday.

"WHAT DO YOU MEAN THE PIZZA PARTY IS GONE?" he yelled. The other bullies shrank back when they saw how angry Robbie was.

"It's the new girl's fault!" said Bill angrily, pointing his finger in Stephanie's direction.

"That's it! No more playing mister nice guy," Robbie growled as he walked toward Stephanie.

Mrs. Gouche entered the room and called the class to order. That quieted things down, but not for long. As Robbie went to the back of the room to hang up his backpack, he "accidentally" knocked all the papers off my desk. As I bent down to pick them up, he whispered harshly into my ear. "You and your nerdy friends have had it!"

"Had what?" I asked innocently, prompting Robbie to plant a huge dusty footprint on my social studies assignment. He might have been doing me a favor.

Maybe the dirt would cover up some of the grammatical mistakes and misspelled words on the paper I had written on the Louisiana Purchase.

As Robbie hung up his backpack, he "accidentally" knocked Justin's off the hook, sending it crashing to the floor with a loud thud. Mrs. Gouche looked up from her desk but didn't say anything.

Justin's backpack is always filled to the top. He always has three or four books, but he also carries a wide assortment of other things, depending on what he's thinking about when he packs it. One day there may be a Frisbee, because he's trying to figure out what makes them fly so well. On another day, it may be his Rubik's Cube (he's working on his own solution but still has to rely on an instruction book to solve it). There could be a ball of string, or a harmonica, or the pair of x-ray glasses he bought at the magic shop so he could see who was knocking on his bedroom door (they didn't work, of course, but he still put them into his backpack sometimes). Once he even had two bricks, and when I asked him, he couldn't remember why they were in there. I sort of wished that the backpack had fallen on Robbie's foot, since Justin probably had something heavy in it.

As Justin, Stephanie, and I sat together in the cafeteria at lunch, Robbie and the other bullies decided to join us. Lunch immediately went from break time to torture time.

"What are you eating, shorty?" Robbie taunted Justin. "Did your mommy pack you something good?"

Justin started to reply, then thought better of it and just continued to eat his sandwich in silence. He was probably hoping that Robbie didn't see that his mother had cut the crusts off the bread. There would be no end to the teasing if they noticed that.

"Yum, cookies!" Bryce said as he snatched a couple of Oreos from my lunchbox. Like Justin, I decided to just let it slide. Sometimes the best way to handle bullies is by not letting them know they're getting to you.

But sometimes they keep it up anyway.

"What's the deal with the pizza party?" Robbie asked Stephanie.

"Easy come, easy go," she said, looking directly into his face. "You wouldn't have had the pizza party in the first place if it wasn't for me, so you're no worse off now, are you?"

Robbie's face began to turn red, and we braced for his response. He took a couple of deep breaths and rose from the table. When he was standing, he towered over us. He bent over the table and stared intently at Stephanie.

"You better find a way to get that party back," he threatened. He picked up her milk carton and slowly poured it into her lunchbox, soaking her sandwich, Goldfish crackers, and carrot sticks.

"Or else!" he added as he and the other bullies stomped away.

"Well, that was a pleasant lunch," Stephanie said as she watched the gang dump their trash and head out to the playground.

"You and I definitely have different definitions of pleasant," I said.

For the rest of the week and into the next, the tension between Stephanie and Mrs. Gouche continued to build. The teacher barked at Stephanie several times, and Stephanie barked right back. The result was twice as much homework as usual. Normally I liked to do math homework, but Mrs. Gouche was really piling it on. I also noticed that it was a lot more difficult than usual.

Justin had finally had enough. When Mrs. Gouche went over to work with the blue math group, he glared at Stephanie.

"What are you trying to do?" he asked in a harsh whisper.

"Well, she was wrong," Stephanie replied. "There are at least two better ways to solve that problem."

"And you're always right, aren't you?" Justin said snidely.

Between the bullies, Mrs. Gouche, and Justin and Stephanie arguing, I was glad to hear the three o'clock bell ring. I'd had enough school for one day. Stephanie didn't walk home with us. I saw her up ahead walking with a couple of girls from her soccer team. Justin and I walked home together, but neither of us had much to say. Our problems at school were beginning to mount, and we didn't have a good solution to solve any of them.

When I reached my house, I tried to open the front door, but the doorknob wouldn't budge. It was locked. I dug through my pockets and emptied my backpack onto the front porch, but there was no key. I slumped to the ground and leaned against the house in frustration. This was the second day in a row I had forgotten my house key. Of course, it had to happen on the day that my mom volunteered at the food bank and my sister had cheerleading practice. I snorted at the thought of a bunch of middle school girls with pompoms dancing around and yelling with absolutely no clue about any of the sports they were cheering on. At least Stephanie actually played a sport. In fact, from what I could see at recess, she was really good— better than most of the boys in the class. It took away from some of her time with the Math Kids, which was a little irritating, but I guess not everyone wants to do math all the time like I do.

So there I was, stuck on my front porch, waiting to see who would be the first one in my family to get home. In the past, we had hardly ever locked our doors, except maybe when we were going away on vacation or to visit my grandma in the next town for a couple of days. But that was before the burglaries. They had been going on for over two weeks now, and our parents were a little on edge.

I overheard them talking about it a few nights ago when they thought I was concentrating on my video game.

I like to play video games, but I'm not obsessed with them like Justin. He plays for hours every day and is an expert at every game he's ever played. I usually get bored with a game long before I get any good at it. I guess I'd rather be solving a tricky math problem than jumping over things, shooting aliens, or finding hidden coins.

"Do you think it's safe here?" my mom asked.

"I'm sure the police will catch the burglars soon,"

my dad replied, but there was a touch of doubt in his voice. I knew he was bothered because the police didn't seem to be making any progress.

"I worry about the kids," my mom said. She and my dad were in the kitchen, and their voices carried into the family room where I sat on the floor with a bag of potato chips next to me and a game controller in my hand. She would reprimand me later for leaving crumbs on the rug, but for now, she had other things on her mind. I crept to the doorway so I could hear better.

"They'll be fine," my dad said, catching me looking at him and throwing a wink my way. "Jordan's getting lots of practice out there killing zombies so I'm sure he'll be able to protect us."

I grinned at my dad, but I could see that he was worried too.

It was the same story with my friends. Justin's parents used to let him stay home by himself, but now they hired a babysitter every time they left the house without him. My sister's friend Amy stayed with him a couple of times during the week, and Justin hated it.

"They treat me like I'm eight years old," he complained one day as we were walking to school.

To be fair, Justin had been eight years old just a few months earlier, but I wasn't going to remind him of that. Instead, I said "My sister treats me the same way."

Actually, although I complain about her a lot, she doesn't treat me too badly overall. Mostly she ignores me, which was just fine with me. Justin is an only child, so his parents are very protective of him.

The only good thing that had come out of this for Justin was that his parents had given him a cell phone so they could check in on him if he wasn't at home. For his parents, it was peace of mind. For Justin, it meant he could play video games wherever he was.

On Saturday, I had gone over to Stephanie's house to work on some of the math homework Mrs. Gouche had assigned. It had poured all morning, so Stephanie's soccer practice had been cancelled. Justin couldn't come over because he was stuck running errands with his parents.

Stephanie and I had made good progress on the homework when we heard her mom and dad coming down the stairs. We weren't exactly trying to spy on their conversation, but we lowered our voices so we could hear them better. I think our parents get so used to us being loud that when we're quiet they don't even realize we're there.

"Maybe we should have stayed in California," Stephanie's mom said.

I could only make out part of her dad's response because of the clinking of dishes as he emptied the dishwasher, but it sounded like he agreed. Then we heard him say, "I could talk to my boss and see about getting transferred back."

Stephanie looked shocked. *Would they really move back just when she was getting settled in?* I wondered. *What about her soccer team? What about the Math Kids?*

Her face scrunched up with worry. I'm sure my face was a mirror image of hers. Parents don't always notice, but when they worry, we do too.

CHAPTER 7

The tension between Justin and Stephanie continued to boil under the surface of our math group like red hot magma in a volcano. I was waiting for the eruption, and on Wednesday morning it finally came.

Mrs. Gouche had spent the morning English class teaching us about the different parts of speech. I had nouns and verbs figured out, but she lost me when it came to adverbs and adjectives. Stephanie and Justin seemed to pick it up easily, but I looked on in frustration.

"Okay, Jordan, in this sentence, which word is the adjective?" Mrs. Gouche asked, pointing at the sentence she had written on the board.

The big dog jumped quickly through the door.

"Quickly?" I said with absolutely no confidence.

"Are you asking me or telling me?" she asked with a smile.

"Telling you?" I asked, drawing laughter from my classmates.

"Stephanie, can you help Jordan out here?" the teacher asked.

"The adjective is *big*," Stephanie said, before going on to explain. "An adjective describes a noun. *Quickly* is an adverb, since it describes a verb."

"That's correct," Mrs. Gouche said. "Does that make sense, Jordan?"

I nodded, but I still didn't get it. Luckily, it was time for PE class, so thoughts on the parts of speech faded as I walked out of the classroom.

We were doing a six-week unit on soccer, so we met Coach Harder on the playground.

"Okay, same teams as last week," he yelled.

I wasn't really into soccer much, and neither was Justin, so we stood at midfield and talked.

"*Quickly* is an adverb, since it describes a verb," Justin said, mocking Stephanie.

"I think she was just trying to help."

"Well, I think she was trying to show you up," he said firmly. "She thinks she's so good at everything."

There was a cheer as our team scored. I saw several people giving Stephanie high fives, so I guessed she had been the one to put the ball into the net. She looked in our direction and a slight frown crossed her face.

Coach Harder blew his whistle and everyone stopped.

"Do you two want to join the game?" he yelled. We looked around for a moment before we figured out he was talking to us.

We lined up on our side of the field, but still weren't paying much attention when Stephanie stole the ball from Susie and passed it to Justin. The ball bounced off his leg and right into the path of Bryce, who barreled toward the goal. Justin and I, who were supposed to be on defense, stood flatfooted.

"Come on, guys! Get in the game!" she shouted as she rushed back to defend the goal. She wasn't fast enough though, and Bruce scored, putting his team up by three.

We half-heartedly joined the play but were glad when the coach gave his whistle three hard blasts to signal that PE was over and it was time to go back to class. Justin and I were walking together when Stephanie appeared in front of us, her hands firmly planted on her hips and a look of exasperation on her face.

"We could have won that game if you guys had helped a little more," she scolded.

"Who died and made you coach?" Justin asked.

"I'm sorry that I like playing a game that doesn't involve trolls and zombies," she shot back. She turned her back on us and walked away.

"Big deal. You can kick a ball with your feet. Try something that requires your brain," Justin said, stopping Stephanie in her tracks.

"And your video games require your brain?" Stephanie asked, turning to face Justin.

"Actually, they do," he said. "There's all kinds of math involved in video games, as a matter of fact. Computer programmers design whole worlds using math equations. You wouldn't understand because all you do is run up and down a field."

"You don't know anything about soccer, Justin," she

said angrily. "There is so much more to it than just running up and down a field and kicking a ball. You want some math? How about geometry? A soccer field has rectangles, circles, and arcs. A soccer ball is made up of twenty hexagons and twelve pentagons. Where a goalie positions herself is all about computing angles so she can block the shot. Think of the math involved in two people running down a field and passing a ball. We have to worry about two different running speeds, the position of the defenders, and the distance between us in order to calculate the angle and how hard we need to kick the ball. And I'll give you one more: there's something called the Magnus effect. It's what makes a soccer ball curve when you kick it the right way. Try programming that into your stupid video game!"

Justin was quiet, and this time, I was pretty sure I could guess what he was thinking. He was thinking about all the math that went into a soccer game and how maybe he had read Stephanie wrong.

She wasn't finished though.

"And I'll tell you one more thing about soccer, Justin. It's a lot more than running and

kicking a ball. It's about working together. It's about teamwork. It's about having each other's back when the going gets tough. That's what soccer is about and that's why I love it."

With that, she turned and stomped into the building, her ponytail bouncing with each step.

Justin remained silent as he watched her walk away.

CHAPTER 8

"A my came to watch me again last night," Justin said the next day at school. "Although mostly she just sat on her phone and talked to your sister." I could tell he wasn't happy with the situation.

"I wish they'd catch whoever it is that's been robbing the houses," I said. "Joe said that the police were looking at a lot of clues."

Joe Ponnath is a year behind us in school, and his dad is a sergeant in the police force. The burglaries were a big topic at school, and Joe was enjoying being in the spotlight. Even the fifth graders were paying attention to him. At recess, there was a crowd gathered around him asking him questions about the robberies. I don't think he knew much about them really, but he wasn't going to let anyone else know that.

"The police are looking for one guy, but my dad thinks it might be an entire gang," Joe said to the crowd. "He said we need to be careful because they could be armed and dangerous."

I wondered if his dad had really said anything about the criminals being armed. I think Joe was just glad to have someone pay attention to him, so he needed to make it seem as if he knew everything about the case.

"The chief of detectives is even thinking about calling in the FBI," he said, drawing some *oohs* and *aahs* from the crowd, especially the younger kids. The FBI? That was big league!

"Does your daddy have to go running to the FBI every time he can't solve a simple crime?" asked Robbie.

Joe started to defend his dad, but then wisely shut his mouth when he saw Bryce and Bill standing behind Robbie. Joe was a scrappy little kid and didn't mind fighting with the older kids, but he wasn't about to take them on when he was outnumbered three to one.

"I bet my dad could find those lousy robbers in no time," Robbie bragged. Robbie's dad is also a police officer, but his job is mostly giving out tickets to people who don't put money in the parking meter. Still, no one in the crowd dared to ask why Robbie thought his dad would be able to crack the case. When Robbie talks, it's sometimes good to just listen to him and not interrupt with things like facts.

Stephanie isn't one for taking good advice though, and she decided to speak up. I think part of it was because the bullies had been picking on her ever since she had bet and lost the class pizza party.

"If he's anything like you, your dad couldn't find him if he was wearing a big sign that said *robber*," Stephanie said, putting her hands on her hips defiantly.

The crowd went silent. The younger kids stepped

back quickly. The older kids pushed forward. They wanted to see if Robbie would hit a girl. The look on Robbie's face said that he wouldn't have a problem doing just that. He stepped toward Stephanie with a sneer.

"You better take that back," he said.

Stephanie stood her ground. "I'm not taking anything back," she said.

Robbie took another step forward. He was now standing right in front of her. She still didn't move.

"First you lose us our pizza party, and now you're insulting my dad?" Robbie asked. "That's a good way to get your face rearranged."

"So it'll look like yours?" she shot back.

That was it. She had gone too far. Robbie raised his fist and took aim at Stephanie's face. I was hoping that the end-of-recess bell would ring or that one of the teachers would step in, but it wasn't either of those that saved Stephanie.

It was Justin.

Before Robbie could throw a punch, Justin stepped in between them. The top of his head barely reached halfway up Robbie's chest, but there he was standing toe to toe with him!

"First of all," Justin began, "Stephanie didn't lose us a pizza party. In case you forgot, she was the one that won the party in the first place. Second, I'm getting really tired of picking up my backpack from the floor every time you knock it off the hook."

Robbie was looking at Justin's forefinger poking him in the chest in amazement. So were the rest of us.

"And third—" Justin was cut off by the recess bell ringing loudly.

Robbie gave Justin a good hard push. Justin managed to stay on his feet, but just barely.

"This isn't over," Robbie said as he turned to walk back toward the building. "I'll see you after school."

Stephanie and I stared after Robbie, then turned to Justin.

"That was amazing," Stephanie said.

"That was crazy!" I said. "Have you lost your mind?"

Justin just stared off into the distance. The second recess bell rang, letting us know we were going to be late getting back to class.

"We need to solve it," Justin said.

"Solve what?" Stephanie asked.

"The case. We need to solve the case," Justin replied.

"The burglaries?" Stephanie asked.

"Yes. If we can solve the case, we'll be heroes," Justin said.

I let that thought sink in to my head. Justin was right. We would be heroes if we could figure out who was robbing the houses and put an end to it. It would also mean Stephanie wouldn't move back to California, Justin wouldn't need a babysitter, and I wouldn't be locked out of my house again.

"But how are we going to do it if the police can't?" I asked.

"Math," said Justin confidently.

We couldn't get any more out of him because Coach Harder was yelling at us to get back to class.

On the way, Stephanie asked the question I wanted

to ask. "What was the third thing you were going to tell Robbie?"

Justin grinned. "I don't have a clue. I was making it up as I went along. I figured that if I talked long enough, the recess bell would ring."

"Well, I definitely owe you one," Stephanie said.

"Nope, we're a team," Justin replied with a grin. "That means we've got each other's backs."

Stephanie smiled.

I was glad that Justin and Stephanie had patched things up, but I still had a lot to think about that afternoon. How were we going to solve a police case using math? How was I going to get Stephanie back on Mrs. Gouche's good side? Most importantly, how was I going to get Justin safely past Robbie and his gang after school without getting us all beat up?

Every time I looked over at Robbie, he was staring at Justin. Whenever Justin looked up, Robbie would slam his fist into the palm of his other hand and point at him. This wasn't looking good for Justin. I had to think of something and quick.

Normally, Robbie wasn't a problem after school since he was stuck in detention. Unfortunately, Robbie had managed to stay out of trouble this week, and none of the teachers had seen him push Justin at the end of recess. To save Justin, I needed to come up with a way to get Robbie in trouble, even if that meant sacrificing myself. Hey, what are friends for?

While Mrs. Gouche was writing our social studies homework on the board, I wadded up a sheet of paper and threw it at Robbie's head. It missed, soaring over him and smacking into the side of Bryce's head. Bryce turned toward the direction of the shot and stared directly at Robbie. Wadding up his own paper, he fired a shot at Robbie, which bounced off his desk and hit Bill. That started a chain reaction, and the next thing I knew, there were balls of paper flying all over the room. Mrs. Gouche turned around and her eyes focused on Robbie crumpling up a large sheet of construction paper he had taken down from the wall.

And that was it. Justin's problem was solved, at least for today. Robbie, Bryce, and Bill were headed back to detention, and we would have safe passage home.

On the way home, we stopped at Stephanie's for a snack. I wanted to find out how Justin thought we could solve the burglary case.

"It's easy," he said. "We just need to get our hands on the clues."

Little did we know, getting our hands on the clues would turn out to be the easy part.

CHAPTER 9

After talking with Joe Ponnath, we ended up having our next Math Kids meeting at the police station. Joe's dad was working on Saturday, and he agreed to sit down with us for a half hour to share some of the clues. I was a little surprised a police detective was willing to discuss the case with us, but Joe had explained to his dad that Stephanie and Justin had stood up for him at recess.

"What kind of information are you looking for?" Detective Ponnath asked.

"Well, we're trying to see if maybe there is a pattern the thieves are following," Justin explained. "If so, maybe we can use some math to figure out where they might hit next."

Detective Ponnath chuckled. "Solving crimes is what we do for a living, Justin," he said. "Do you really think you can find something we've missed?"

Justin thought about the question and then responded. "Sometimes, when I'm working on a hard math problem and get stuck, I'll talk to Jordan about it," Justin explained. "What I find a lot of times is that I'll end up coming up with a solution just by talking through the problem with him."

Detective Ponnath nodded. "Not a bad idea," he said. "Okay, let me tell you what we've got. There have been seven robberies and two more attempted robberies. The latest one was three nights ago," he started.

"Could you go through them in the order that they happened?" Justin asked. "That might help us to figure out if there is a pattern."

As usual, he had asked just the right question.

"I can't get into all of the details," Detective Ponnath explained, "but most of this information is public knowledge already, so it should be okay to share." The detective went through the burglaries in order, giving us the dates and addresses of the break-ins, as well as the items that were stolen. Justin took notes while the detective talked.

"Wow, that's a lot of clues," Stephanie said when Detective Ponnath had finished.

"Not really," Detective Ponnath said. "These guys are very smart. We don't have any witnesses. No one saw any strange cars in the neighborhood. We don't have any physical evidence. No fingerprints, so we're pretty sure they are wearing gloves. No shoe prints. Nothing left at the crime scene that can help us to identify the suspects."

"But maybe there's something here," said Justin thoughtfully. "Maybe there's a pattern that we're missing."

"Well, if you think of something, please let me know," said the detective. "People are really scared and we need to catch these guys."

"Why do you think it's more than one person?" I asked.

"Great question, Jordan," he responded. "At the last robbery, they stole a big screen television that was too big for one person to carry. That's why we think there are at least two of them."

We thanked the detective and headed for home. On the way, we stopped at the library and used the copier to make duplicates of Justin's notes so we would all have them.

"I'm sure there's some kind of pattern here," Justin said.

"Maybe, but I don't know how we're going to find it if the police can't," I said.

"Maybe it's like Stephanie adding up the numbers from one to one hundred," Justin said. "Maybe we just need to think about it a little differently than the police."

"What do you mean?" Stephanie asked.

"Well, we were trying to add the numbers one at a time because that's the way we've always done it," said Justin.

"So?" I asked.

"So, the police are used to looking for things like fingerprints and shoe prints and license plate numbers because that's the way they've always done it," Justin said. "We've got to look at it a different way."

"But if the police don't have any evidence, how are we going to catch the crooks?" Stephanie asked.

"We'll just have to catch them in the act," Justin said.

"How are we going to do that?" I asked.

"We're going to think like a criminal," Justin said with a smile. "More importantly, we're going to think like a criminal who doesn't want to be caught!"

Justin didn't say any more after that. I could tell he was deep in thought as we walked home. He was looking at his notes like he thought the answer would jump right off the page if he stared long enough.

I was hoping the Math Kids were going to be able to start working on solving the burglary case right away, but Stephanie had a soccer game. Justin looked a little irritated when she said she had to go, but he didn't say anything. Stephanie cut through the Greenfeld's back yard to get to her house on Iowa Street. It would have been a little quicker to go through the Watsons' yard, but the Watsons had two giant Doberman Pinschers who looked like they'd love to have a fourth grader for a snack. My sister was friends with Janet Watson and said the dogs were really pretty nice, but I didn't want Stephanie to be the one to find out if she was wrong.

"I can't believe she thinks soccer is more important than solving this case," Justin said.

"She's really good though," I said in her defense, drawing a frown from Justin.

"So? Who cares about soccer?" he said.

I decided to keep my opinion to myself. Justin is my best friend, but he can be a little judgmental sometimes. I wondered what he would think if I said something about all of the video games he plays.

When we got to my house, I asked Justin if he wanted to come in to start looking at the clues, but he just said "Mm-hmm" and continued walking to his house.

That left just me. I poured a glass of milk and grabbed a handful of cookies from the pantry. Sitting at the kitchen table, I looked down at the information Detective Ponnath had given us, all of it written down in Justin's neat handwriting.

1) Sept 2nd – 13 Main Street
2 TVs and jewelry
2) Sept 3rd – 29 Third Street
Money and a stereo
3) September 5th – 71 Fifth Street
Crooks stole purse off kitchen table
4) Attempted robbery on September 7th – 47 Seventh
Neighbors heard dogs barking at 9:30 pm
Police called but nothing stolen
5) September 7th – 59 Seventh Street
Money and jewelry
6) September 11th – 101 Walnut Street
Money, jewelry, and TV
7) September 13th – 149 Oak Street
Purse, wallet, laptop

8)   Attempted robbery September 17th – 19 Maple
House broken into but nothing stolen
Large German shepherd in house
9)   Robbery on September 19th – 3 Washington
Street
Big screen TV

Seven robberies and two attempted robberies in a little more than two weeks.

As it turned out, the thieves weren't done yet!

CHAPTER 10

The thieves hit again the very next night. That brought the total number of robberies up to eight. Detective Ponnath was right. These thieves were smart! Even with extra police patrols all over town, there were still no eyewitnesses to any of the robberies.

My parents were worried because it looked like the robberies were getting closer to our own house. The latest robbery was on Ohio Street, only seven streets away from ours.

My parents were planning to have a small dinner party on Saturday. They had invited Stephanie's parents to introduce them to the neighborhood, and Justin's parents were supposed to come too.

There was one problem though. With the latest robbery striking so close to home, my parents were thinking of cancelling their party.

I called a special Monday meeting of the Math Kids. If we were going to solve the case, we needed to do it quickly!

We met at Justin's house after school. Everyone looked very serious. This wasn't like my sister's seating chart. This was a real problem. Where would the robbers strike next? And when?

"What do you think, Justin?" I asked.

I could tell Justin had already put a lot of thought into the problem. His notes from the police station were marked up with circles joined by red lines and arrows. More handwritten notes had been added.

"I think there's something there, but I haven't figured it out yet," he admitted. "They keep moving farther away from the river, but I'm not sure if there's a pattern or not."

Justin pointed to a map that he'd taped to the wall. He had large red *x*'s showing where every robbery or attempted robbery had taken place. The *x*'s showed that the robberies had started near the river and were moving farther away each time. Unfortunately, that meant they were moving closer and closer to our own houses, which Justin had put on the map too.

The streets in our town were laid out in groups of streets with similar names. The first robbery was on Main. That was followed with three robberies on what we called the *number* streets. There was one on Third, one on Fifth, and one on Seventh. The next three robberies were on the *tree* streets: Walnut, Oak, and Maple. Then there were two on the *state* streets: Washington and, the latest one, on Ohio. That's how we knew the robberies were getting close to us. Stephanie lived on Iowa Street and Justin and I were on Missouri Street.

I explained the street layout to Stephanie.

"All we know is that the crooks are headed in our direction," I said.

"I think we may know more than that," Justin responded.

Stephanie and I looked at Justin, waiting for him to explain.

"Except for the first two robberies, they always skip at least one street in between robberies," Justin said.

I looked at the map and saw that Justin was right. Maybe there was a pattern after all.

"It might help if we numbered the streets in the order the robberies happened," I said. I took the marker from Justin and started to add numbers down the left side of the map, beginning with the number 1 on Main Street where the first robbery happened.

The robberies had taken place at streets numbered 1, 2, 4, 6, 10, 12, 16, 18, and 22.

"Does anyone see a pattern in those numbers?" I asked.

"Before you answer, can I ask a question?" Stephanie said.

"What is it?" I asked.

"There's a Third street, but no First or Second. How come?" she asked.

"They renamed them to Riverfront Drive and Main Street," I said.

"Then I think we should start the numbering with Riverfront Drive," she said, never taking her eyes off of the map.

"Why?" I asked. "The first robbery was on Main Street."

"Trust me. I think I might see something," she said.

I crossed out my numbers and restarted with Riverfront Drive as number 1.

1	Riverfront Drive
2	Main Street ✖
3	Third Street ✖
4	Fourth Street
5	Fifth Street ✖
6	Sixth Street
7	Seventh Street ✖ ✖
8	Eighth Street
9	✖ Ninth Street
10	Tenth Street
11	Walnut Street ✖
12	Beech Street
13	Oak Street ✖
14	Birch Street
15	Sequoia Street
16	Aspen Street
17	Maple Street ✖
18	Pine Street
19	Washington Street ✖
20	California Street
21	Mississippi Street
22	Virginia Street
23	Ohio Street ✖
24	Florida Street
25	Louisiana Street
26	Texas Street
27	Colorado Street
28	Nevada Street
29	**Stephanie** → Iowa Street
30	**Jordan** → Missouri Street ← **Justin**

"Look at all the streets where the robberies happened," Stephanie said excitedly.

I looked and started naming the streets, "Main, Third, Fifth—"

"No, not the names. Look at the numbers!" she exclaimed.

I started again, "Okay, we have 2, 3, 5, 7, 11—"

This time it was Justin who interrupted. "That's it!" he grabbed the marker and started stabbing it at the numbers in excitement.

"What's *it*?" I asked.

"The robberies happened on streets 2, 3, 5, 7, 11, 13, 17, 19, and 23," he said. "Notice anything about those numbers?"

"They're all prime!" I said. "They're all prime numbers!"

"That's right," Stephanie said, her ponytail bobbing as she nodded her head with enthusiasm.

"But couldn't that just be a coincidence?" I asked.

"Maybe," Justin agreed.

"I don't think so," Stephanie said.

"Why?"

"Look at the dates of the robberies," she said. "The robbery on Main Street, what we're calling street 2, happened on September 2nd."

"And the robbery on street 3 was on September 3rd!" Justin added.

We went back and checked every single one, and sure enough, every street number matched the date when the robbery happened. That couldn't be a coincidence! The crooks had a pattern. That means we could figure out when and where the next robbery would take place.

"The last robbery was on the 23rd. The next prime number after that is 29, so if they keep following the pattern, that means the next robbery will take place on September 29th," Justin said.

"That's this Saturday!" I shouted.

"And that means the street will be the 29th street," Stephanie said. She counted six streets past Ohio. Her eyes got very wide. "That's my street!" she said.

We all looked at each other. We knew where and when the robbers were going to hit next, but what were we going to do about it?

CHAPTER 11

We had a hard time focusing on school for the rest of the week. Robbie and his band of merry morons continued to bother us whenever they could. Justin's backpack spent more time on the ground than it did on its hook. We started eating lunch right next to the cafeteria monitor so we wouldn't be bothered. We kept our eyes open for the bullies when there weren't any adults around. To make matters worse, Mrs. Gouche continued to pile on the homework in our math group.

None of that mattered though. We needed to figure out a plan for Saturday night. But first, we needed to figure out exactly where the crooks were going to hit.

"Too bad the clues didn't show us which specific house they were going after," I said as Justin and I walked to the cafeteria for lunch on Wednesday.

"I think they did," said Justin. "Well, maybe not the exact house, but at least a way to narrow it down."

"Did you find something?" I asked.

"Yes," Justin said. He started to explain, but our path was suddenly blocked by Robbie and Bill.

"Your little girlfriend cost us a pizza party," Robbie growled.

"She's not my girlfriend!" Justin shot back.

"I saw you passing notes to her today," Bill said.

"That was math homework," Justin said, but I knew the note was really about the burglaries because I had passed it to him.

"Wow, you really are a nerd," Bill laughed. "Even your love notes are about math."

"It wasn't a love note!" Justin said. I could tell he was starting to get mad. His face was turning red and his fists were clenched by his side.

Robbie stepped forward, and Justin backed up until he was pressed against the wall. I looked around for a teacher, but there weren't any in sight.

"You better get us our pizza party back, or instead of a date with your little girlfriend, you'll have a date with my fist," Robbie said as he waved his clenched fist in front of Justin's face.

"Is there a problem here, Mr. Colson?" asked Principal Arnold as she came around the corner and saw Justin backed up against the wall.

"No problem, Principal Arnold," Robbie replied as he backed away from Justin.

"Everything okay, Mr. Grant?" asked the principal.

Robbie gave Justin a threatening look.

"Everything's fine, ma'am," Justin replied.

"Then let's get to the cafeteria," Mrs. Arnold said. "Now, Mr. Colson!" She watched as Robbie and Bill walked down the hallway, then turned to us. "Are you sure everything is okay?" she asked Justin again.

"Yeah, everything's fine," Justin said.

We followed Robbie and Bill down the hallway, while Mrs. Arnold kept a close watch on us.

Because of the argument with Robbie, we didn't have time to discuss Justin's ideas on the burglary until school was over. Stephanie, Justin, and I stayed in the classroom while everyone else left, except the bullies, who hung around in the hallway waiting for us until Old Mike shooed them away.

Justin was at the white board with a marker.

"What did you come up with, Justin?" I asked.

"They're all primes!" he said excitedly.

"We already knew that," I said. "If you start from the river, all of the streets are prime numbers."

"No, the house addresses are all prime too," he said. He referred to his notes as he wrote the addresses on the board.

13 Main
29 Third
71 Fifth
47 Seventh
59 Seventh
101 Walnut
149 Oak
19 Maple
3 Washington
23 Ohio
??? Iowa

Stephanie and I checked the numbers and Justin was right. All of the addresses were prime!

"That can't be a coincidence," Stephanie said. "It looks like when these burglars came up with a plan, they stuck with it."

"I think they were trying to be smart by deliberately choosing a pattern that looked random," agreed Justin. "That way the police wouldn't be able to figure it out."

"Now what do we do?" I asked.

"We know the day. We know the street. Now we need to figure out the house," Justin said.

Stephanie was very quiet. She looked troubled.

"What's wrong, Stephanie?" I asked.

"I live at 31 Iowa Street," she said quietly.

Her house address was prime. That meant the crooks might be targeting her house for their next robbery!

"Okay, we don't know for sure that it's your house" I said. "We need to find out all of the houses that have prime numbers on your street."

It didn't take us long to find out. We just had to walk the length of her street. We only had to look at houses on one side of the street since the house numbers on the other side were all even, and we knew there were no even prime numbers except for the number 2.

There were nine houses on Stephanie's side of the street. Justin wrote the numbers down as we walked from one end to the other. He crossed out the house number that were not prime.

21, 23, 25, 27, 29, 31, 33, 35, 37, 39

That left only four possible choices, including Stephanie's house.

"I think we can narrow it down even more," Justin said. "The burglars don't like dogs, so I think the Watsons' Dobermans would eliminate number 29."

"And the house near the end of the street, number 23, is empty," said Stephanie. "It's for sale and the family has already moved to their new house."

Justin crossed off the two houses we had eliminated.

~~21~~, ~~23~~, ~~25~~, ~~27~~, ~~29~~, 31, ~~33~~, ~~35~~, 37, ~~39~~

"It's going to be our house," Stephanie said quietly, pulling on her ponytail.

"How do you know it won't be number 37?" I asked.

"The Millers are having a family reunion this weekend," she replied. "I talked to one of the twins, and she told me they have relatives coming in from four states. The burglars would be crazy to try to rob them with all those people around. They'd never get away with it."

We let the truth sink in. If we were right, the burglars were coming to rob Stephanie's house this Saturday night!

And we still didn't have a plan.

CHAPTER 12

On Thursday morning we were no further ahead with a plan. And my parents were still going ahead with their dinner party for Saturday night, which meant Justin's and Stephanie's parents would be at my house for the evening. That meant that Stephanie's house would be empty, with nothing to stand in the way of the burglars.

"We have to do something," Justin whispered to me while Mrs. Gouche was writing on the board.

I glanced back at Stephanie. She was chewing on the end of her ponytail.

At recess, Justin was confronted by Robbie again.

"You better come up with a pizza party by next week or you're toast," Robbie said, waving his big fist in Justin's face.

In our afternoon math group, Mrs. Gouche only made things worse by assigning us a big math project to finish by Monday. She was really piling it on. We complained about the extra work, but at least she was giving us some interesting problems to solve.

That afternoon, we snuck out the back door of the school and made a run for it before the bullies could figure out where we were. Once we were in the clear, we slowed to a walk.

"It's not really a big deal," I said. "All we have to do by Monday is finish a giant math project, find a way to get the class a pizza party, and stop burglars from robbing Stephanie's house."

"Piece of cake," Justin said with a grin. "While we're at it, why don't we throw in a cure for all diseases?"

"And world peace!" Stephanie added.

We went to Stephanie's house after school. Over cold glasses of milk and a large plate of brownies, we talked about what we could do. Food always seemed to help when we had heavy thinking to do.

"I don't see a way we can get our class pizza party back," I said. "So let's concentrate on the math project and protecting Stephanie's house."

"That makes sense," Stephanie replied, but I could see she was still very worried. It was her house that was going to be robbed after all.

"I've got a stupid baby sitter on Saturday night," Justin complained.

"Who is it?" I asked.

"It's Amy again."

"What about you?" I asked Stephanie. I knew with all the adults at my house that I would be stuck in my room for the evening.

"I don't know yet," she said. "I think my parents were planning to ask your sister to sit for me on Saturday night."

"But if we're all going to be in different houses on Saturday night, there's no way for us to stop the burglars," I said glumly.

"Maybe there is," Justin said, "and we have Mrs. Gouche to thank."

Stephanie and I looked at him, waiting for him to explain.

"What if we all had to meet at Stephanie's house on Saturday night?" he asked.

"How would we work that out?" I asked.

"The math project," Justin said. "What if we had to work on the math project? That would give us a good excuse to all be together at Stephanie's house."

"Yeah, but our parents are all worried about the robbers. They'd never let us stay alone," I said.

"But what if we weren't alone?" he asked.

You could almost see the plan taking shape in Justin's changing facial expressions.

"I thought Amy was babysitting you on Saturday," I said.

"Right," said Justin. "And who is Amy's best friend?"

"Of course!" I said, beginning to understand. "Linda owes me for helping her out with her dinner party seating."

"So if we get Linda and Amy to babysit for the three of us—" Justin began.

Stephanie jumped in. "—and we use our math project as an excuse to get together at my house—"

"—we might just pull it off!" I finished.

As it turned out, that part of the plan was easy. Amy and Linda said they would love to babysit together. I didn't even have to use Linda's IOU to get her to agree. The parents were all in agreement too, since now there would be two teenagers watching over us. And how much trouble could we get in while working on a math project?

Now we needed to come up with the important part of the plan. If the robbers were coming, how were we going to catch them?

Our first ideas were terrible. Justin wanted to hang a net from the ceiling and drop it on the burglars. Stephanie thought we could pour super glue on the doorknobs so their hands would get stuck when they tried to come in. My idea wasn't any better. It involved digging a pit in the backyard and putting a pile of money on a trap door for bait.

We all laughed at our silly ideas, but we weren't getting any closer to coming up with a real plan.

"What if we just call the police as soon as they try to break in?" Stephanie asked.

"That might work, but what if they get away before the police arrive?" I asked.

"And if they find out we've figured out their pattern, they'll just start back up again with another pattern and we'll be back to square one," Justin added. "We need the police to catch them in the act."

Stephanie and I talked about a couple of other ideas, but Justin had gone into his thinking zone again. He answered "mm-hmm" a few times when we asked him questions, but I could tell he wasn't really listening to us.

By the time Stephanie's parents got home from work, we still didn't have a plan. Walking home with Justin, I could tell that he was still deep in thought. When we got to my driveway, I asked him what he was thinking about.

"I think I may have an idea that could work," he said. "I still have some details to work out though, so give me a day or two to think it through."

A day or two? That was all the time we had left!

CHAPTER 13

Friday was here. If their pattern held, it meant there was only one more day until the crooks would try to rob Stephanie's house. Justin was quiet the whole day, not even saying much in our math group. He didn't say a word during lunch, not even an "mm-hmm" when I asked him if he had worked out his idea.

At recess, he wandered off by himself, still deep in thought. I lost track of him while I was playing soccer with some of the third graders. I didn't see him anywhere around when the first bell rang. I did see Stephanie though. She was at the far end of the soccer field, talking to Robbie. The other bullies weren't around, but that didn't really matter since Robbie was much bigger than Stephanie. I started to go over to see if I could help, but the second recess bell rang, and I was herded toward the school door. When I looked back, Robbie was shaking his finger in Stephanie's face. Uh oh, this looked like trouble.

Stephanie and Robbie were both ten minutes late getting back to class after recess. I was glad to see that she looked fine. No blood and no bruises anyway. She even had a slight smile on her face. Robbie had a big grin too. I wondered what was up. Something definitely wasn't right.

Stephanie had a dentist appointment that afternoon, so she left class before I had a chance to talk with her about her run-in with Robbie.

I walked home with Justin.

"Any ideas for what we should do tomorrow night?" I asked.

"Not yet, but I'm sure we'll come up with something," he said. He didn't sound very confident though, which was unusual for him. He was used to always having the answer.

I picked at my dinner that night, even though we were having one of my favorite meals, fried chicken with mashed potatoes and sweet corn. The chicken was cooked to perfection, but I just nibbled at the golden-brown crust.

"Is something wrong, Jordan?" my mother asked.

"Well, it's just," I began, then stopped before spilling everything. My mom was now looking at me intently, worry on her face. I hated to see her look so concerned, so I started again.

"You see...it's just that...you know," I stammered.

"Speak much English, dork?" my sister interjected.

"Linda, how many times have I told you about calling your brother names?" my mother snapped.

"About a million," I answered, sneaking a grin at my sister.

In a way, I had my sister to thank for keeping me quiet. I wasn't very good at keeping secrets. Without her, I probably would have told my parents everything, and I knew exactly what would happen then. My parents would call off their dinner party and go straight to the police. If that happened, I was sure the police would end up scaring the crooks away and the burglars would never be caught.

After dinner, I tried working on the math project a little but found I couldn't concentrate. I tried reading, watching TV, and playing video games, but nothing seemed to work. In less than 24 hours, we would all be at Stephanie's house, and outside that house, would be crooks attempting to break in. That was pretty scary stuff, and I couldn't get it out of my head. I called Stephanie's house, but no one answered the phone.

I went to bed around nine o'clock, but I didn't fall asleep for a long time. When I finally did fall asleep, I was troubled by dreams where dozens of robbers were coming into my house through every door and window.

When I woke up, it was Saturday morning. I poured a bowl of cereal, but it didn't seem to have any taste.

"Are you sure you're feeling alright?" my mother asked.

"Yeah, I'm fine," I said, quickly shoveling a big spoonful of cereal into my mouth to prove it. My full mouth also prevented me from saying any more.

She looked at me with a raised eyebrow but didn't ask any more questions.

I called Justin but got no answer. No answer at Stephanie's house, either. Stephanie was probably at soccer practice, but where was Justin? I looked at the clock. It was 9:15. We were scheduled to go to Stephanie's house at five o'clock. That meant there was less than eight hours to go and we still had nothing.

I spent most of the day working on our math project so I wouldn't drive myself crazy.

"You ready to go, Jordan?" my sister asked.

I looked up in surprise. It couldn't be time to go already. I looked at the clock and saw it was almost five o'clock.

"Yeah, I guess I'm ready," I said.

"Wow, you sure sound like you're excited," she said sarcastically.

I started to walk out of the house through the mud room.

"Aren't you forgetting something?"

"Forgetting something?" I responded.

"Uh, yeah, aren't you supposed to be working on some stupid math project?"

I hit my fist into my forehead. Of course. The math project—our cover story. I scooped my papers up and shoved them into my backpack.

"Thanks," I muttered.

"Well, you're sure in a lousy mood."

She was right, but at least I had a good excuse. Once we got to Stephanie's house, we might all be in danger.

CHAPTER 14

There we were. Saturday night. Six o'clock. According to the weather report, the sun would set at 7:30 pm. According to Detective Ponnath, the burglars always hit after dark, so we still had a little time, but that time was running out quickly.

Amy and Linda were in the other room, deep in conversation about the big break-up between Brad and Beth. I wondered if that meant we would have to help her with another seating chart, but we had other things to worry about right now.

"Did anyone come up with anything?" I asked.

Stephanie and Justin shook their heads no, but I noticed that they exchanged a small smile. I felt a little left out of something, but I wasn't quite sure what that something was. I decided not to ask. I was just happy they were getting along. We ate some mac and cheese for dinner and tried to play a board game, but we mostly watched the clock.

Outside, the sky darkened. It would be fully dark in twenty minutes. I looked out of the back window nervously. Justin was trying to look calm as he played with his cell phone. Stephanie nibbled at her pinky finger as the light faded.

Amy and Linda had gone downstairs. We were hiding in the pantry, where we could clearly see through the kitchen to the back door. The house was mostly dark, with only a lamp from the living room around the corner providing a small sliver of light. In our minds, every sound or moving shadow was a burglar. I was sure the small shed in the back yard held nothing more than a lawn mower and some random garden tools, but to me, it was just another hiding place for a crook.

The clock hit 8:30. My parents' dinner party would be over at 10:00. That only left us an hour and a half. After that, we would have to give up and tell our parents what was going on. I could hear music playing softly in the basement, but my heart was pounding out its own beat.

There was a sound at the back door. At first, I thought it was my imagination playing tricks on me, but then I heard it again. It was a scratch and then what sounded like a whisper. It was happening, just like we had predicted. We had solved the problem, but for once, I wished we had been wrong. The doorknob wiggled a little, and the whisper became words as they drifted through the open window over the sink.

"It's unlocked," said the first voice.

"Okay, let's make quick work of this. Grab anything you see that is worth anything. Cash, jewelry, electronics, whatever you can find," came a second voice.

The police were right. There were two of them.

The doorknob slowly turned, and the door inched open with a quiet creak. A hand, covered in a black glove, reached into the opening, widening it until a face peered into the room. At least, I think it was a face. It was hard to tell because, like the hand, it was covered in black.

Stephanie put her hand over her mouth to hold in a gasp. She was tugging nervously at her ponytail with the other hand, but I was too scared to even move. We were deep in shadow, but they would surely see us when they came in. The door was now opened wide enough for the first crook to squeeze into the room. The second followed closely behind.

"Okay, we're in," said one robber. "Looks like no one is home. Ouch!" there was a loud bump as he stumbled into the corner of the kitchen counter. "I think it's safe to use the flashlight."

This was it! When he turned on the flashlight, there was no way they were going to miss the three of us crouched against the pantry wall. I felt Justin squirm a little. A beam of light came on. In seconds, we would be seen.

Suddenly there was the sound of a loud dog barking.

I let out a little yelp, but not nearly as loud as that of the burglar with the flashlight. He backed quickly away, tripped over a chair, and hit the ground with a loud thud and a cry of pain. The other burglar was already on his way out the door.

"FREEZE! POLICE!" came a loud yell from outside. The escaping burglar was framed in the brilliance of a powerful spotlight.

The first burglar was still scrambling backwards trying to get away from the barking. The second burglar was pushing his way back in to get away from the police. They collided in the doorway and crashed to the floor. Stephanie turned on the lights, and I was finally able to see what was going on.

The two crooks were down on the floor. Standing over them in the back door was a large policeman holding a gun. Next to me, Justin was grinning and holding up his phone, which was still blasting the sound of a large dog barking. He pushed a button to silence it.

Justin and Stephanie high fived each other. I just looked on in amazement as the policeman handcuffed the two burglars.

"Perfect timing, Mr. Colson," said Stephanie to the policeman.

Mr. Colson? Robbie's dad?

"Mr. Colson?" I asked her. "I don't get it."

Stephanie explained. "It's simple, really. We had two problems to solve. We needed to catch the burglars—"

"—and, more importantly, we needed to make sure Robbie wasn't going to rearrange my face," Justin finished with a smile.

"So, we found a way to solve both problems at one time," Stephanie said. Like Justin, she had a huge grin on her face.

"So your conversation with Robbie on the playground…?" I was beginning to understand.

"I was telling him that we had come up with a way for his dad to catch the burglars in the act," Stephanie said. "Since we couldn't dig your money pit, Jordan, we needed a policeman."

"And the barking?"

"I knew the burglars were afraid of dogs since they had been scared away from at least two houses that had dogs," Justin said. "Stephanie doesn't have a dog, so I brought my own!" He held up his phone. "In case you were wondering, it's a Golden Retriever. They have the loudest recorded bark, according to the *Guinness Book of World Records*."

I laughed. Not only did Justin think of having a dog ready to go, he had even researched which one had the loudest bark.

I didn't have time to ask any more questions, because Linda and Amy rushed through the basement door.

"What's going on?" Linda asked in alarm.

"Oh, not much," Stephanie replied.

We all laughed while Linda and Amy looked at each other in confusion

CHAPTER 15

T he Math Kids got together again the next day. We wanted to celebrate our success in capturing the burglars. We clinked our glasses of milk together and then plowed into a large plate of Oreos.

"I still can't believe what we did," Stephanie said.

It was amazing. We were just kids, but we had cracked a case that even the police couldn't solve!

Justin explained that it had been Stephanie who had come up with the plan to get Robbie to tell his dad what we had discovered.

"I thought if Mr. Colson got the credit for solving the case then maybe Robbie would leave Justin alone," she explained. "I don't know if that part of the plan will work, but I do know that Detective Ponnath was pretty impressed with Mr. Colson. Hopefully, having a hero for a father will make Robbie back off a little."

Fat chance, I thought, but I hoped she was right.

"But why didn't you guys let me know what was going on?" I asked.

Justin and Stephanie looked at each other.

"Justin said you weren't very good at keeping secrets," said Stephanie.

I looked at Justin.

"Don't you remember that time in first grade when you told Mrs. Becker that I put the frog into the aquarium?" Justin asked. "Or in second grade when you told your sister we were going to leave school early to go to the comic book store. Or in third grade—."

"Okay, okay, I get it," I laughed. I was too happy about our success to be hurt.

It didn't take us long to find out if the bullies were going to back off. Before school had even started the next day, Bill had knocked Justin's backpack off his hook and onto the floor. I guessed the bullying was going to continue.

That's when something amazing happened. Robbie got up from his desk and picked up Justin's backpack. He brushed it off and placed it back on the hook. Justin looked on in stunned silence.

"Hey, man, it looks like you dropped your backpack," Robbie said.

"Thanks," Justin said.

"Don't mention it," Robbie said with a smile. "Happy to help."

The day continued to surprise us. At lunchtime, when we would normally line up to head to the cafeteria, Mrs. Gouche made an announcement.

"Class, we have some guests."

Our mouths dropped open when we recognized the two men who walked through the door. It was

Detective Ponnath and Mr. Colson. Each carried a stack of pizza boxes. It turned out we were getting our pizza party after all!

"This is just a little thank-you for your classmates who helped us to capture the burglars," Detective Ponnath said with a large smile. "Come on up here, kids. Stephanie, Justin, Jordan, and Robbie!"

Robbie?

I started to say something, but Justin whispered, "Just let it go, Jordan."

Justin was right. It didn't hurt to let Robbie get a little credit for talking his dad into hiding in the tool shed while we waited for the burglars. And if it would give us a little break from him and the other bullies, it was well worth it.

"What a great day," said Stephanie as she stuffed her face with pizza.

"Almost perfect," agreed Justin.

"Almost?" I asked.

"Well, we didn't get that math project done," Justin said. "Hopefully, Mrs. Gouche will give us a couple of extra days to finish."

"Maybe we don't need more time," I said. I went to my desk and pulled out a neatly-stapled stack of papers. Justin started to read, flipping through the pages as he began to smile.

"You finished the project!" he said.

"Well, someone had to do the math work while you guys were wasting all your time plotting how to catch criminals," I smiled.

"We make a great team, don't we?" Stephanie said.

"We sure do," Justin agreed.

"To the Math Kids!" I yelled, holding up my box of chocolate milk.

Justin and Stephanie touched their own milk boxes to mine.

As we drank our milk and celebrated our success, I couldn't help but wonder where our math club would take us next.

THE END

COMING SPRING 2019! A SEQUENCE OF EVENTS, BOOK 2 IN THE MATH KIDS SERIES. DON'T MISS IT!

The Math Kids Club is back! After solving the case of the prime-time burglars, The Math Kids, Jordan, Justin, and Stephanie, are ready to return to the original purpose of their club: solving math problems. And the district Math Olympics is the perfect opportunity to do just that. But before they can enter the competition, they need a fourth teammate. The Math Kids set their sights on Catherine Duchesne.

Even though Catherine has been quiet in class, she knows some really cool math tricks that are sure to help The Math Kids win the competition. But when Catherine doesn't show up for school and Jordan, Justin, and Stephanie find out her father's been kidnapped, the group springs into action to help their new friend.

WANT TO DO MATH LIKE THE MATH KIDS?

ADDING THE NUMBERS FROM 1 TO 100

The amazing thing about Stephanie adding up the numbers from 1 to 100 is that the story is true. Okay, there was no pizza party. There was also no calculator, since the story happened before calculators had been invented. And the teacher's name probably wasn't Mrs. Grouch either. So, what part of the story was true? Carl Friedrich Gauss was eight years old when his teacher gave the class that assignment back in 1785. Carl really did come up with the correct answer of 5,050 after only a few seconds of thought. The teacher—and the rest of his class—was amazed that he could do it so quickly.

How did he do it?

Well, Carl wasn't just any eight year old. He became one of the most famous mathematicians in the world (sometimes he was even called the "Prince of Mathematicians"). One of the reasons Carl became so good at math is that he didn't look at numbers the same way as everyone else. Most people would look at those numbers like this:

1, 2, 3, 4, 5 ... 98, 99, 100

IF YOU'RE NOT FAMILIAR WITH "..." IN A LIST OF NUMBERS, IT JUST MEANS TO KEEP GOING IN THE SAME PATTERN. IT IS CALLED AN ELLIPSIS. MATHEMATICIANS ARE LAZY SOMETIMES, AND IT'S EASIER TO WRITE "..." THAN IT IS TO WRITE OUT ALL 100 NUMBERS.

Carl Gauss looked at the numbers a little differently though. He thought of what it would look like if he stacked the numbers from 1 to 100 on top of the same numbers from 100 down to 1.

1	2	3	4	5	...	98	99	100
100	99	98	97	96	...	3	2	1

He then noticed a helpful pattern to the numbers when he added the rows of numbers together.

$$1 + 100 = 101$$
$$2 + 99 = 101$$
$$3 + 98 = 101$$
$$4 + 97 = 101$$
$$5 + 96 = 101$$
$$...$$
$$98 + 3 = 101$$

$$99 + 2 \quad = 101$$
$$100 + 1 \quad = 101$$

Carl saw that he had 100 pairs of numbers that all added up to 101, so he multiplied 101 x 100 to get 10,100. He then divided that number by 2 to get 5,050. Why did he divide by 2? Because he was adding each number twice, he knew he had to divide the total by 2 to get the right answer.

Was that the only way Carl could have quickly solved the problem? No, there are actually at least three or four other ways he could have done it. All the methods of quickly solving the problem all have something in common though. They all look at the numbers a little differently. That's what *The Math Kids* series is all about. It's about looking at numbers a little differently. In fact, it's about looking at math a little differently—looking past adding, multiplying, subtracting, and dividing and seeing math as something that's not boring, but actually very cool.

THE BRIDGES OF KÖNIGSBERG

The Bridges of Königsberg is a classic math problem that was given to a famous mathematician named Leonhard Euler about three hundred years ago. It involves an area of mathematics called graph theory.

The old town of Königsberg has seven bridges. Can you walk through the town, visiting each part of town and crossing each bridge only once?

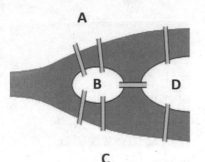

A

B   D

There are four areas of town.
We'll label them A, B, C, and D.
There are seven bridges.
We'll label the bridges 1 to 7.

C

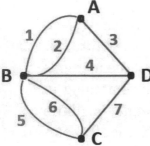

We can simplify this picture
even more. In mathematics, this is
called a graph.

In a graph, each point (A, B, C,
and D) is called a *vertex*.

Each line (1 to7) is called an
edge.

The number of edges which end
at a vertex is call the *degree*.

There are 3 edges (1, 2, and
3) ending at vertex A, so we say
vertex A has degree 3.

If we can start at any vertex and draw a line that
goes through every vertex (A, B, C, and D) and along
each edge (1 to 7) without lifting our pencil, we've
solved the problem. The path that we draw is called an
Euler path.

Here's what that would look like with some easier
shapes:

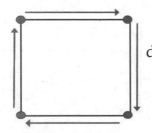

This shape has 4 vertices, each with
degree 2.

We can draw an Euler path.

This shape has 4 vertices, two with degree 3 and two with degree 2.

We can draw an Euler path if we start at either of the vertices with degree 3.

We can't draw an Euler path if we start at either of the vertices with degree 2.

This shape has 4 vertices, all with degree 3.

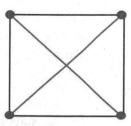

We can't draw an Euler path. That means we can't draw this shape without lifting up our pencil.

Euler figured out that we could tell which graphs have an Euler path by counting how many vertices have an odd degree (1, 3, 5...).

We can only draw an Euler path if the number of vertices with an odd degree is 0 or 2.

If there are two vertices with an odd degree, the Euler path must start and end at the vertices with an odd degree.

So, how could the Math Kids have quickly figured out if they could solve the Bridges of Königsberg problem? All they had to do was to count the vertices with an odd degree!

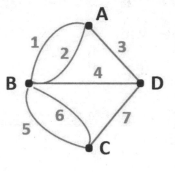

In the Bridges of Königsberg graph there are 4 vertices with an odd degree (A, C, and D have degree 3 and B has degree 5).

Since there are more than two vertices with an odd degree, there is no way to draw an Euler path.

In other words, there is no way to walk through all areas of the town and go over each bridge just one time.

PRIME NUMBERS

Prime numbers are natural numbers that can only be divided by 1 and itself. What is a natural number? It is an integer greater than zero. These are sometimes called the counting numbers. If a number can be divided by another number (besides 1 or itself), it is not a prime. Two is a prime number because the only numbers that can divide it are 1 and 2. Four is not a prime number because it can be divided by 2. Two is the only even prime number because all other even numbers can be divided by 2.

How can we find out if a number is prime? A long time ago, a Greek mathematician named Eratosthenes of Cyrene, came up with a way to quickly find prime numbers. The method is called the sieve of Eratosthenes.

A sieve is like a strainer you use to drain the water out of a pot of spaghetti. The sieve keeps the numbers that are prime and drains out all the numbers that aren't.

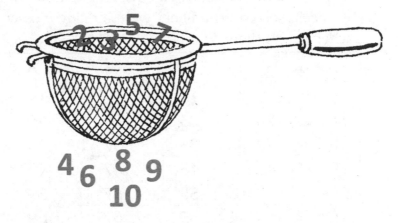

Let's look at the first hundred numbers. Eratosthenes started with the number 2, which he knew was prime. He then crossed out all multiples of 2 (all even numbers) because he knew they couldn't be prime.

	2	3	4	5	6	7	8	9	10
11	12	13	14	15	16	17	18	19	20
21	22	23	24	25	26	27	28	29	30
31	32	33	34	35	36	37	38	39	40
41	42	43	44	45	46	47	48	49	50
51	52	53	54	55	56	57	58	59	60
61	62	63	64	65	66	67	68	69	70
71	72	73	74	75	76	77	78	79	80
81	82	83	84	85	86	87	88	89	90
91	92	93	94	95	96	97	98	99	100

The next number not crossed out is 3, so that is also a prime. Eratosthenes then crossed out all multiples of 3. Some numbers, like 6 and 12, are multiples of both 2 and 3, so those numbers were already crossed out when he got there.

	2	**3**	4	5	6	7	8	**9**	10
11	12	13	14	**15**	16	17	18	19	20
21	22	23	24	25	26	**27**	28	29	30
31	32	**33**	34	35	36	37	38	**39**	40
41	42	43	44	**45**	46	47	48	49	50
51	52	53	54	55	56	**57**	58	59	60
61	62	**63**	64	65	66	67	68	**69**	70
71	72	73	74	**75**	76	77	78	79	80
81	82	83	84	85	86	**87**	88	89	90
91	92	**93**	94	95	96	97	98	**99**	100

The next number not crossed out is 5, so that is also a prime. Eratosthenes then crossed out all multiples of 5.

	2	**3**	4	**5**	6	7	8	9	10
11	12	13	14	15	16	17	18	19	20
21	22	23	24	**25**	26	27	28	29	30
31	32	33	34	**35**	36	37	38	39	40
41	42	43	44	45	46	47	48	49	50
51	52	53	54	**55**	56	57	58	59	60
61	62	63	64	**65**	66	67	68	69	70
71	72	73	74	75	76	77	78	79	80
81	82	83	84	**85**	86	87	88	89	90
91	92	93	94	**95**	96	97	98	99	100

The next number not crossed out is 7, so that is also prime. He crossed out all multiples of 7.

	2	**3**	4	**5**	6	**7**	8	9	10
11	12	13	14	15	16	17	18	19	20
21	22	23	24	25	26	27	28	29	30
31	32	33	34	35	36	37	38	39	40
41	42	43	44	45	46	47	48	**49**	50
51	52	53	54	55	56	57	58	59	60
61	62	63	64	65	66	67	68	69	70
71	72	73	74	75	76	**77**	78	79	80
81	82	83	84	85	86	87	88	89	90
91	92	93	94	95	96	97	98	99	100

The next number not crossed out is 11, so that is also prime. He found there weren't any multiples of 11 to cross out because they had all been crossed out already. Eratosthenes knew he was done because 11 x 11 is bigger than 100. That means all the numbers that hadn't already been crossed out were prime numbers.

	2	**3**	4	**5**	6	**7**	8	9	10
11	12	**13**	14	15	16	**17**	18	**19**	20
21	22	**23**	24	25	26	27	28	**29**	30
31	32	33	34	35	36	**37**	38	39	40
41	42	**43**	44	45	46	**47**	48	49	50
51	52	**53**	54	55	56	57	58	**59**	60
61	62	63	64	65	66	**67**	68	69	70
71	72	**73**	74	75	76	77	78	**79**	80
81	82	**83**	84	85	86	87	88	**89**	90
91	92	93	94	95	96	**97**	98	99	100

ACKNOWLEDGMENTS

Writing a book isn't easy, and it certainly isn't done in a vacuum.

First and foremost, I want to thank Common Deer Press for taking a chance on a guy with a crazy dream of writing a children's series with a math theme. Thanks, Ellie Sipala, for stepping out on a limb for me. I know it was a seriously thin branch, and I will always be grateful for you sharing my vision.

Thanks to Kirsten Marion, who made the whole editing process so easy. I hope you know that I couldn't have done this without your thoughtful ideas and your incredible enthusiasm for the story. You made this a much better book.

Thanks also to the rest of the team at Common Deer Press: Emily, Siobhan, and Anastasia. Publishing a book is a real team effort, and I couldn't ask for a better team!

Thanks to Shannon O'Toole for her excellent artwork. You really brought The Math Kids to life and now I can't picture them looking any different.

Thanks to all of you who read through my painful first attempts at this book and provided such great feedback.

Tom Winter, Chasity Wickenhauser, and the MathNerds@Facebook group: thanks for the early read by your kids. Their thumbs-up kept me going when I wasn't sure if kids would like what I was writing. Special thanks for early reads by Shannon Clarkin, Stephanie Peace, and Justin Cole. I appreciate your suggestions and also that you were able to provide your criticisms without shattering my fragile ego. Thanks to my friend Mark Fauser, my writing inspiration who always reads anything I send his way. Who loves you, buddy?

To my own Stephanie, Jordan, and Justin, you are my continual inspiration. A dad couldn't ask for better kids.

To Debbie, who deserves so much better than I could ever give her but stays by my side nevertheless. I love you for that and so much more.

ABOUT THE AUTHOR

*D*avid Cole has been interested in math since was very young. He pursued degrees in math and computer science. He has shared this love of math at many levels, including teaching at the college level and coaching elementary math teams. He also ran a summer math camp for a number of years. He has always loved to write and penned a number of plays which have found their way on stage. David had always wanted to combine his love of math and writing, and now with The Math Kids, he has done just that! He feels that writing about math is a great way to exercise both sides of the brain at the same time.

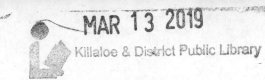